Capitol in Crisis

Capitol in Crisis

Kathy Roy Johnson

RESOURCE *Publications* · Eugene, Oregon

CAPITOL IN CRISIS

Resource Publications
An Imprint of Wipf and Stock Publishers
199 W. 8th Ave., Suite 3
Eugene, OR 97401

www.wipfandstock.com

PAPERBACK ISBN: 978-1-7252-6845-6
HARDCOVER ISBN: 978-1-7252-6846-3
EBOOK ISBN: 978-1-7252-6847-0

Manufactured in the U.S.A.   09/25/20

Excerpts of Psalm 118 are from the Revised Standard Version (RSV)

I dedicate this book to Carol June Hooker
whose friendship and guidance helped me write this book.

I also dedicate this book to my husband, Ed,
who regularly makes laugh and daily teaches me to love!

Acknowledgments

MY LIFE IS BLESSED with friends, many of whom made this book possible. First and foremost, I want to thank Carol June Hooker who's helped me throughout the production of this book with countless hours of editing, plot discussions, and cajoling. I also want to thank Barry Casey, who edited this manuscript and gave me invaluable advice during this process. Ellen Masciocchi, my lifelong friend and fellow writer, shared tips and ideas which improved the quality of this work. Likewise, Kathy and Jack Thomson provided me with advice and insights which strengthened the book. Betty Phifer explained some of the intricacies of fire and rescue. My guardian angel, Chris Daley, gave me creative ideas throughout this process! Thanks also goes to Debbie Reinsch, my dear friend who helps me laugh—especially at myself.

I also wish to acknowledge my family, especially my brother-in-law, Doug Hollmann, along with his wife, Linda Odoughda, who have helped me understand the complexities of transforming a story into an actual book. My beloved nieces, Megan Hollmann Fantinelli and Catherine Hollmann, have encouraged me throughout this process.

Thanks also go out to Pastor Don McFarlane, Pastor of Administration at Sligo Seventh-Day Adventist Church, for his review of the book. Likewise, Dr. James Londis, longtime friend, teacher, and theologian, reviewed the book and provided some helpful pointers.

Finally, I want to thank Mike McCurry, Director of the Center for Public Theology at Wesley Theological Seminary for graciously agreeing to review my book. I was privileged to work with Mike on Capitol Hill many years ago and I am honored by his assessment of this work.

Of course, I want to thank Wipf and Stock Publishers for helping me transform this work into an actual book!

Finally, I thank my husband, Ed, for loving me and believing in my creative ability.

Prologue

FAR BELOW THE U.S. Capitol, there is a sub-basement, with bare cast-iron pipes in the ceiling and exposed brick painted a drab institutional yellow. Dusty old boxes containing long forgotten reports line the hallway, awaiting their demise. An elevator shaft stands at one end of the hall, unused for decades. Abandoned desks and mismatched chairs add to the clutter. No one frequents this hallway, with the exception of a few maintenance men who require access to the mechanical room. The other end of this hallway adjoins a larger corridor leading to a small café about fifty feet away. Well known for its superb coffee, this little café has only a handful of tables and decidedly limited seating. Like the old boxes and furniture, it seems out of place. Nevertheless, for busy Congressional staffers and an occasional member of Congress, it offers solace, its gentle proprietor a welcome respite from the rough-and-tumble world of politics.

Recently, the Maintenance Department designed and installed a new electrical system in the mechanical room to improve the heating system of the Capitol. Considered a minor change, only a handful of workers even know about the installation of this new system. It should be a simple thing to accomplish. The crew chuckled at the notion that management felt it would take two full days to install the new system.

"It's a minor change." they argued. "We'll be finished in half a day. Nothing to it."

Yet even minor changes can sometimes have unintended consequences.

ADDIE HUTCHISON FINISHED MAKING the last sandwich and lined up the lunch bags in a neat row. The large pot of oatmeal began to boil while she finished frying the link sausages and added them to a platter with several slices of toast.

"Y'all better come and eat now. It's 6:15. I'm not playing games this morning. You boys gonna worry your Gran into the grave!"

Addie tried hard to get her boys fed and ready for school by 6:30 sharp. Actually, they were not "her boys." Rather, Tyrone, aged fifteen, and the twins, James and Jamal, aged eight, were Addie's grandsons. She'd been raising the boys on her own ever since a drunk driver killed her daughter and son in-law. Two years had gone by, but it seemed like yesterday. Addie tried not to think about that too much: it left such an awful hole in her heart. Sorrow had been Addie's companion for a long time, but she kept her smile and her gentle countenance about her.

She was about to call for them again when James and Jamal tumbled into the kitchen.

"Mornin' Gran. Man, am I hungry! Guess I'm growing', huh?" Jamal had such a sweet face, she found it hard to discipline him, even when he needed it.

"Gran, how much do basketball players make? Because that's what I'm gonna be someday. I'll have a big house and a pretty wife." James grinned. "You'll live with us too, Gran!"

Just then Tyrone came into the kitchen, his tall, lanky frame barely clearing the entrance. He brushed Addie's cheek but avoided eye contact.

"Good morning," he mumbled, dropping into place at the table.

Before they touched their food, they all bowed their heads as Addie prayed, "Loving Lord Jesus, thank you for this food and this new day. Please be with those less fortunate than us and please guide these boys today in their studies and keep them safe. Amen!"

As the boys began devouring their food, Addie looked intently at Tyrone. "Honey, you feeling all right? You look tired. I noticed you been sleeping well past 6:00. You're always up by 5:30."

"I'm fine, Gran," he responded as he shifted in his seat, avoiding her gaze. "Maybe I'm getting lazy. You better be getting on now, Gran. You know how you hate to miss your bus. I'll take care of these guys."

Addie was grateful: Tyrone always walked the twins to school. It meant she could get to work on time. She reached for her coat, picked up her purse, and said, "You boys behave in school and do your work. Jamal, the Lord gave you one mouth and two ears: you listen today, honey. James, work on that spelling list because even basketball players need to spell.

"Tyrone, please lock both doors."

Addie had to hurry to make the bus, but she was smiling as she heaved her round body up the steps to the fare booth. She grinned at the driver, an old friend of many years. He scolded her good-naturedly, "Miss Addie, you know good and well I ain't gonna leave you!"

"Sam, you're one of my guardian angels, now that's the truth."

Addie sat and gazed out the window as the streets slipped past. The neighborhoods were changing: cleaner streets, expensive cars, higher prices. Soon enough the bus reached Capitol Hill and she made her way to the café.

Addie always arrived at 7:00 a.m. sharp, even though the shop didn't open until 7:30. This mystified her colleagues, family, and friends.

"Girl," they said, "why do you get up so early? That's just stubbornness is what that is."

Addie let them talk and smiled: she had her reasons. She took pride in her work. She considered it an honor to run a shop in the U.S. Capitol. After working for Senate Food Services for thirty-two years, Addie took over the coffee shop which was nestled under the Capitol within a complex series of tunnels, connecting the Senate to the House. She took pride in that little shop, and she ran it with a firm hand and a gentle heart. Her coffee was known as the best on the Hill, although Addie never divulged her secret—chicory, with a dash of cinnamon.

She hummed an old hymn as the silver urns hissed and burbled and a rich aroma of fresh coffee filled the small café. She shifted the tables into neat rows and bent to pick up some litter. In a moment she would open the doors and the steady barrage of customers would begin. The first wave would be the Congressional staffers rushing in for their quick fix on the way to work. She took one last look around, making sure things were neat and tidy. Then, she unlocked the door and took her seat atop the high stool in front of the cash register.

⌒

Simone Perez bent to tie her running shoes, pulled on her fleece jacket, and stepped outside her front door. For several moments she stood stretching on the stoop of her Georgetown home in the early dawn, her body silhouetted against the morning sky. The cool October air made her shiver as she bounded down the stairs and sprinted west toward Massachusetts Avenue, rhythmically pacing her steps. Soon, a sheen of sweat soaked her face. She faithfully adhered to her running regimen. At least one part of her day would always be predictable.

For several minutes she thought of nothing except the cadence of her steps as her shoes slapped the pavement. Gradually, she allowed herself to take in the sights and sounds of Washington, D.C.—her new home. She jogged in place at a light, relishing the morning air. The light turned green, and Simone resumed her run, her black ponytail swishing back and forth as her dark eyes took in the edifices that lined Massachusetts Avenue, each distinctive building telling a story. An architect by trade, Simone longed to stop running and study each structure. But alas, that would have to wait, as she had enough on her plate.

As the newly-appointed Architect of the Capitol, she was responsible for the operation, development, and preservation of 17.4 million square feet of buildings. Everything from the Botanical Gardens to the U.S. Supreme Court complex fell within her purview. Frankly, the sheer magnitude of her responsibilities sometimes left her speechless. Not that Simone was any shrinking violet. She enjoyed a wide acclaim among fellow architects. Quite unexpectedly, the search committee had approached her about the position. She'd been teaching at Tulane University, and those who knew the work she'd done restoring portions of New Orleans after Hurricane Katrina referred to it as stunning. Simone could never understand why she'd received such accolades: she was just doing her job.

As she approached Chevy Chase Circle, All Saint's Episcopal Church came into view. She slowed her pace to a power walk, remembering another chapel and another time in her life. Strange how her memories of her time at St. Anthony's Catholic Church and orphanage still haunted her, even now. She vividly recalled nuns who expected absolute perfection; Simone never felt she measured up. Many of the nuns were kind, and she had received a top-notch education. Still, the little girl grew up telling herself constantly, "I must do better." Deep within her heart, she had never quite felt adequate.

Simone glanced at her watch and picked up her pace. Sprinting the last few yards down her block, she took the steps to her door at a bound, pleased she'd completed her morning routine. Inside, she showered quickly and dressed in a tailored gray suit and powder-blue silk blouse. Simone Perez possessed a beauty all her own. She wore her thick black hair pulled back in a bun that snuggled neatly in the nape of her neck. With her high cheek bones and tall slender body, she drew admiring glances. Yet, as she blotted her lipstick, she frowned at herself in the mirror.

Simone believed in being punctual and well-prepared for meetings. She had five today, including lunch with an old friend. She needed to gain a working understanding of the Federal budget process, and Rodger Haskins, the Administrator of the General Services Administration, had promised to guide her through it. Then the Speaker of the House, John McIntyre, had asked her to stop by at 4 p.m. to talk about some renovations to the Cannon Building. He seemed to be a kind man, she mused, but still he always made her nervous. She couldn't say why.

She glanced at her watch and sighed, realizing she was running late for her 8:00 meeting. She'd hoped to grab a cup of coffee and chat with her friend Addie about some new recipes she discovered over the weekend. Simone couldn't decide which displeased her more; missing her Monday morning chat with Addie or having to settle for the weak, bland coffee served in her office.

Exasperated, she grabbed her briefcase and headed for her car.

Bruce Graham rushed through the tunnel, vowing not to be late today. As the Chief of Staff of the Senate Judiciary Committee, he was about to preside over the most important hearing of his career. Dressed in a navy Brooks Brothers suit and a red silk tie, he looked the part. He clutched his thick briefing book under his arm, even though he knew the book cold. Today was the confirmation hearing of Winton W. Davis for a seat on the Supreme Court of the United States. The Senate Judiciary Committee would confirm

Davis. Six months later, Bruce would become the Honorable Davis's Chief Clerk. His career plan was on track.

It wasn't until he was almost at the little underground café in the bowels of the Capitol that he glanced at his phone and suddenly realized the date: October 14. A year had come and gone since he separated from Shelley. After law school they had moved to D.C., and for a while things were normal. Yet as Bruce threw himself into his work, Shelley accused him of ignoring her. They fought regularly for two months, then one morning he found a note next to the coffee pot which said simply, "Bruce; I've moved out. Please don't call. I need some space. I wish things were different."

Three weeks from today his marriage would officially end.

He ducked into the café for a large coffee and a glazed donut. He still had a few moments, he realized. He decided to sit and review his briefing book one last time.

Father Dan Larson, pastor of St. Matthews Episcopal Church of McLean, noted for having a number of members of Congress in its parish, had to play the part. Today he'd be meeting with Congressman John Chamberlin, Chair of the House Ways and Means Committee, to talk about a number of social issues. He managed to smile as he opened the café door.

"Addie Hutchison, I've missed you! It's really great to see you!" He held open his arms.

"I declare, Father Dan!" Addie smiled broadly as she gave him a hug. "How're things at that church of yours? Are you takin' good care of that wife?"

"Addie, I am so lucky to have Colleen. She's my girl! Church is a whole other story. I'm here a bit early this morning. I've got a vestry meeting this evening, and between you and me, I'm not ready. Give me a medium coffee and a bagel." Father Dan reached for his wallet and handed her a five-dollar bill. Then he reached into his coat pocket and slipped her a check.

"That's for you and the boys," he said.

Addie gasped and tears filled her eyes. "Father Dan, you have no idea what this means to me. Raising those boys on my own, I don't know up from down half the time." She shook her head. "They eat like ten grown men! Please, tell your wife how much I appreciate this. We'll come and visit your church again soon, I promise! I'll fix some fried chicken. Lordy, Father Dan, if you weren't married, I'd smooch you here on the spot. Now go! Get yourself ready for your meetin.' Thank you, you hear?"

As he sat down, Dan wished he could offer a prayer over his breakfast. Lately, he'd found it difficult to pray at all. The same old doubts kept him off his knees. They had for quite some time now.

"Ah, if only they knew," Dan thought as he bit into his bagel.

～

Jim Stenson made his way through the House tunnel to his favorite coffee shop, listening as the tap of his cane echoed off the polished concrete floor. As he walked, he tried to count his steps: twenty-one from the escalator to the tunnel, seventy-two from the beginning of the tunnel to the coffee shop. As the Legislative Director for Blind Citizens United, he knew his way around the Hill. Although people were always offering to help him, he was determined to make it on his own.

Tap, tap, tap.

He made the last turn and felt for the door of Addie's café.

"Mornin' Addie! Sure hope you have some of that delicious coffee left." Jim loved this little café.

"Morning, Mr. Stenson," Addie called out cheerfully. She handed him a cup as he paid. "Help you to a table?"

"No, thanks," he responded. "I'll go to my usual corner table."

"Just let me know if you need anything," said Addie.

Jim Stenson knew exactly what was on his calendar today. He was appearing as a witness before the House Education and Labor Committee for several programs serving blind and visually impaired individuals. In the afternoon he had the dubious honor of chairing a task force on the employment of persons with disabilities, as it decided which position to take on a House bill coming up for a vote. Later that evening he'd be speaking at a reception for the inclusion of persons with disabilities in the arts.

Just another ordinary day, he mused.

He opened his computer and brushed his fingertips across the Braille keyboard. He worked quickly and quietly, keeping track of the time, making certain every email received a timely and accurate response.

～

Congresswoman Barbara Perkins's heels clicked as she made her way from the parking garage toward her office. She had stayed up late and risen early, preparing for today. With three big votes scheduled at noon today on the

Defense Appropriations bill, Congresswoman Perkins still had a number of questions for her staff and she wanted them answered well before the vote would occur. She chuckled to herself, wondering why her staff felt it was so important to prepare four-inch-thick briefing books with information she'd probably never use.

I wish they'd just talk to me, she thought.

In truth, this was not the life she'd envisioned for herself. This was her late husband's dream. Congressman Paul Perkins had been a popular Democratic member of the House from Cheyenne, Wyoming, who had represented his district with distinction for eighteen years. There had been many rumors he would make a run for the White House.

Then came that terrible day. They were at home in Cheyenne for the President's Day recess. It had been snowing all night and Paul planned to speak at a meeting of businessmen in Gillette. Barbara had begged him to cancel because of the weather, but he felt he had to go since he was the keynote speaker. He'd take a puddle-jumper, he said, and assured her he'd be home for dinner. Barbara could still see the police chief who came to the door to deliver the news: Congressman Perkins's plane had gone down shortly after takeoff.

"I'm sorry, Mrs. Perkins, but there were no survivors."

That moment remained etched in her memory: no survivors.

Hours—not days—after the tragic accident, Democratic operatives approached Barbara about completing her late-husband's term.

"It will be easy," they had said. "Just put everything on autopilot and preserve Paul's legacy. It's only fourteen months."

Thus, Barbara had assumed her husband's responsibilities. That was five years ago. Now she was in her second term and many in the Democratic Party had big plans for her. It was rumored she would soon become the next Chairwoman of the coveted House Education and Workforce Committee.

She succumbed to her need for coffee. Instead of taking the tunnel which led to the Rayburn House Office Building, she took a right and happily opened the door to Addie's café.

ᕰ

Fred Rafferty and Billy Drexler sat in a small mechanical room. They were installing more electrical connections which could support cogeneration, allowing more efficient use of power and steam to heat and cool the Capitol. Soon, they would complete its installation.

"I don't mind telling you, I'll be really glad when this new electrical system is hooked up. This has been really tough," Fred said to Billy as they set out the tools they'd need. They hoped to complete the cut-over to the new system later that day, and with everything hooked up they just needed the big boss from the Capitol Power Plant to give final approval.

"Man, you're telling me!" Billy said.

Although Fred was ten years older and had extensive electrical experience, Billy served as the liaison for this particular project. He'd been with the Capitol Maintenance Department about a year and this was his first major solo project. Fred was more than happy to assist this eager young man.

"These connections are the most complicated thing I've worked on so far," exclaimed Billy. "I went to school for three months on this dumb thing, and I'm still not sure how it works. Don't even get me started on the brass at the Capitol Power Plant! Those guys are a bunch of flunkies if you ask me. Take today, for instance. They're already half an hour late! "

For a long while both men busied themselves in routine tasks which needed to be completed. Fred could see Billy was becoming fidgety, so he wasn't surprised when he finally blurted, "Fred, I'm not going to try anything stupid, but I want to start some testing of my own. Let me know if you hear anything out of the ordinary."

"Sure, Billy," Fred nodded, and went back to his work.

For a few minutes, all Fred heard was the click, click, click of Billy's electrical gauge as he checked and rechecked the electrical connections.

Billy thought to himself, *Those guys from the hoity-toity Capitol Power Plant must think we have all day. It really burns me up!*

Reaching up, Billy threw a switch and turned to speak. "That should—" He stopped at the look of horror on Fred's face.

"Oh God, no! What have you done! Billy, you just threw the main power switch! The system isn't ready for that kind of voltage. It can't handle it yet!"

Billy spun around and his hands trembled as he tried in vain to turn the switch back to off, but he couldn't override the system. Anxiously, he tried to remember his training, replicating the schematics in his mind. "Come on!" he panted, frantically. The mechanical room was filling with smoke.

Fred, coughing and struggling for breath, smelled the unmistakable odor of burning electrical wires.

9

"I'll radio Dom," he cried. We need help fast!"

He lunged for the walkie-talkie, knocking it to the ground. As it skittered away, he bent down and groped frantically for it in the smoke, knowing every second counted. It slid under a cabinet and he dropped to his knees, feeling for it. Just as his fingertips brushed it, the smoke enveloped him.

Billy screamed, "Fred, let's go!"

He turned to run as the room convulsed violently. In a blur of pipes, water, and falling debris, a deafening explosion threw him across the room. He struggled to stand but saw with horror that his left leg was pinned beneath a huge cast-iron pipe. Worse still, Fred lay motionless in a heap.

A wave of searing pain cascaded through his body and everything went black.

2

Rob Tate was sitting at a small metal desk waiting for a meeting with Dom when he felt the explosion. Immediately, he knew what had happened. A twelve-year veteran at the Maintenance Department, Rob knew things weren't right, and at this moment, things were definitely not right. He stood up from the desk and felt another, more violent, explosion.

"Rob, what just happened?" barked Dom Martinelli, Chief of the U.S. Capitol Maintenance Department for thirty-six years. A physically imposing man, Dom demanded excellence from his staff. If you planned to work for Dom Martinelli, you'd better know your stuff.

Without replying, Rob leaped to his feet and raced out of the room, flying down three flights of stairs.

"Wait, Rob!" Dom yelled, trying to keep up. "We don't know what happened! Maybe it's an earthquake."

"Probably the new electrical system, Dom," Rob shouted over his shoulder as he ran to the basement tunnel. He was flicking through electrical configurations in his mind. His instincts told him something had gone wrong while Billy was calibrating the new line. Perhaps he'd inadvertently crossed the old and new lines. Rob desperately wanted to be wrong. He made the final turn into the basement tunnel on the House side and stopped short. "Please, God no!" Rob's voice cracked.

"This can't be!" Dom exclaimed. A dense wall of rubble stood before them. The basement tunnel had completely collapsed. For a long moment, neither of them could utter a word.

Rob found his voice first. "Dom, let me run to the Senate side and see what's what. Call Security! Tell them I'm coming, and I may need help. Ask somebody to bring me a radio. I'm going to need . . ."

"But Billy and Fred . . ." Dom stood paralyzed.

"Dom let's see how the Senate side looks. It may not be as bad as it appears." Rob didn't wait for Dom's reply. He bolted up the stairs and through the Capitol Rotunda, shouting as he ran, "Maintenance coming through! Make way!"

Tourists gawked as a short, skinny man darted through their path. In moments, Capitol Hill Police Chief, Paul Dupre caught up to him.

"What happened?" Rob ran down the stairs, not even bothering to answer. As they reached the Senate side, Rob held his breath.

There was rubble strewn everywhere, yet the tunnel had not fully collapsed along its 300 feet between the House and Senate chambers. It was impossible to know how many were hurt at this point, but Rob knew he had to get to the mechanical room, no matter what.

"I'll secure the area—this looks pretty bad." Police Chief Dupre turned and ran for the stairs. As he peered around the rubble, Rob could hear the Chief bellowing, "Stand clear! We're closing the Capitol. If you do not have official government business in the Capitol, I must ask you to leave immediately. Let's go, folks!"

Rob picked his way around the pile of bricks and twisted pipes, hoping to reach the mechanical room, but it was no use. It looked like the tunnel had collapsed about twenty feet from the entrance. Through the smoke and dust, Rob could just see the jagged hole where the door had been.

"No!" he shouted, "there's got to be a way to get through."

He turned back toward the House side, mentally reviewing the options. Lost in thought, he had not realized Dom was beside him until he spoke.

"Rob, let's go upstairs and regroup. Maybe we'll find a way to get through."

"Upstairs, Dom?" Rob interrupted. "People may be trapped in that tunnel—and you want me to go upstairs and regroup? We don't have that kind of time. People may be dying! Here's what I'm doing: I'm going to go through the vent space above the tunnel on the north side, where it's probably passable. Maybe we can get some sort of line down to Billy and Fred . . ." Rob's voice trailed off.

"OK," said Dom. "But sooner or later Paul Dupre and Simone Perez are going to need to know what happened, and what the heck we're doing. So, go assess the vent space and then you come back to my office. Fair enough?"

"Yeah, Dom, I hear you," Rob said as he hurried to the vent space.

❧

Simone Perez was sitting in a large conference room for her weekly staff meeting, when the entire building shuddered violently. The vibrations and cracking continued for what seemed like minutes as plaster rained down and coffee spilled across the table. Her staffers scrambled to move laptops, calendars, and notes.

"What the heck?" one of them cried, "It feels like an earthquake!"

For a moment, Simone sat in stunned silence, paralyzed with fear. Her mouth suddenly felt dry, and for a split second she imagined grabbing her purse and fleeing to the solitude of her home. Instead, she sprinted for her office without a word, making a mental list of whom to call as she ran. She was reaching for the phone on her desk when it rang.

"Ms. Perez, this is Paul Dupre with Capitol Police. Look, there's been some kind of an explosion in the House tunnel. We don't think it's a terrorist attack. Dom Martinelli's guys are on it. Apparently, they were installing some new electrical connections in the mechanical room under the Capitol and they might have crossed the lines. The D.C. Fire Chief is on his way. For now, we're evacuating the Capitol. I suggest you and your staff get over to Rayburn till we know it's safe. Then I'll be in touch—"

"Is anyone hurt?" Simone interrupted."

Dupre paused. "There could be fatalities. Keep that under your hat. The press is going to be swarming this place. I need to run, but I'll be in touch within the hour."

"Thanks, Chief."

Simone grabbed her purse and laptop, directing her staff. "Let's go folks—the Chief is evacuating the Capitol for now. This is not a day off. We're heading to Rayburn cafeteria and we'll regroup there. I need a detailed schematic of the tunnel right away! Hurry up."

As she exited the Capitol, she pulled out her cellphone and pressed Dom Martinelli's number. Technically, Dom worked for her.

When he answered she barked, "Mr. Martinelli, this is Simone Perez. What is going on? I want some answers and I want them NOW! I am not fond of the Chief of the Capitol Police knowing more than I do about the Maintenance Department, which I supervise. Do I make myself clear, Mr. Martinelli?"

"Simone—I mean Ms. Perez. My staff is looking into it as we speak. What we do know is there's been some sort of a . . ."

"I know that," Simone interrupted impatiently. "What caused the explosion? Are there fatalities? How many? Are there survivors and if so where? Is the Capitol safe structurally? You see, Mr. Martinelli, there are 535 members of Congress and they will want answers to all of these questions. Therefore, you'd better figure this out now. Oh, and as a special incentive—I want hourly updates from you and your staff, starting at 10:00, when I expect you to participate in an interagency meeting!"

Simone ended the call abruptly and immediately regretted her tone. She made a mental note to speak to Dom later and explain they'd have to pull together and figure things out on the fly.

∾

Earl Bentsen, Chief of D.C. Fire and Rescue, was sitting in his office going over training materials for an upcoming meeting when the first alarm came into the fire station. Nothing unusual there, except it came from the Capitol—and that was *always* a call Earl noticed. The second alarm didn't bother him either. Probably just a simple kitchen fire. When the third alarm sounded, Earl dropped everything and ran downstairs, deftly suiting up before jumping on the fire engine.

"What do we know, Bobby?" Earl shouted to Bobby Jenkins as the howl of the siren rose.

"Chief, there's been an explosion somewhere in the basement of the Capitol," replied Bobby, sliding behind the wheel. "What's unusual is they're requesting backup of the Capitol Police Department, sir. Ambulances are three minutes behind us."

Earl Bentsen had worked for the D.C. Fire Department for thirty-four years. He had come up through the ranks and he knew well what to expect. In truth, very little bothered him. Yet, a three-alarm fire with heavy ambulance backup at the Capitol could only mean injuries and maybe fatalities. Instinctively, he dialed his counterpart at the Capitol Police, Paul Dupre.

"Paul, what's going on over there? You fellas sure know how to kick off Monday morning right," Bentsen joked.

"All I can tell you for sure is we think the explosion came from the mechanical room," Dupre said. "They were getting ready to cut over to a new digital electrical system. I know for sure there are some casualties. Worst thing is, it looks like much of the underground tunnel that connects the Capitol to both the House and Senate collapsed. The subways are fine, but the connecting tunnel is a shambles."

"Understood," Earl replied. "The D.C. Fire and Rescue Services has your back. I'll be on site in four minutes."

The training materials would have to wait.

⌘

The cafe customers lay on the ground in stunned silence, barely able to breathe. Coffee pooled on the floor around shattered glass in the now-darkened café. For a long moment, no one moved. Ceiling tiles dangled and dust hung in the air, making the café look surreal and dream-like. The fluorescent lights from the refrigerator cases emitted an eerie glow and provided a small amount of light to the cafe. Addie lay in a semiconscious state, her head and shoulder throbbing.

She moaned and tried to sit up, calling out weakly, "Father Dan! Are you all right? I . . . I think I need some help."

Father Dan was silent for a long moment, having hit the right side of his head on the cement floor. Finally he said, "I think I'm okay. Give me a moment and I'll try to help you up."

He got to his feet unsteadily and stood, taking deep breaths, and then hobbled over to where Addie lay. He bent down and tried to help her up, but he didn't have the strength. He glanced at a movement to his right and saw a fellow on his hands and knees, searching for something. "I'm Dan," he said. "Can I help?"

"I'm Jim Stenson. I'm blind and I'm searching for my cane. If you'll help me find it, I can help you get Addie up."

Dan hesitated. "Well, here's your cane, but"—

"Dan," Jim interrupted, "I'm blind but I work out regularly and I ran ten miles before work this morning. I can help you, just take me over to her."

Across from Jim, an attractive woman sat up, trying to pull herself together. "What just happened?" she asked in a dazed voice.

Dan offered her his handkerchief. "Hi, I'm Dan Larson."

"Barbara Perkins. I think I'm okay." She turned, "Addie, are you there?"

Addie looked up through the dusty haze, moaning. Turning slowly, she said "Lord, have mercy, what happened? Mr. Stenson are you okay?"

"Yes, I'm fine," Jim responded. "Dan and I are going to help you up."

Dan called over, "You over there; can you help us?"

A well-dressed man looked up tentatively and said, "You're asking me to help get that woman up?"

"Yes," responded Dan.

"I don't think so." He brushed dust from his suit. "I'm going to be late for an important hearing. I'm Bruce Graham, Chief Counsel for the Senate Judiciary Committee."

With that, he picked up his briefcase and made his way through the door, but he quickly returned after realizing the doorway was now a pile of rubble.

"Well, good for you," said Jim Stenson sarcastically.

Dan led Jim to where Addie lay.

"It looks like she has hurt her shoulder. If you can just reach under her left arm and gently pull up at a forty-degree angle," Dan carefully instructed.

"I went to nursing school before I got married, so I at least know the basics," volunteered Barbara. "Someone call 9-1-1!" she said, looking in Bruce's direction.

"You're in great hands, Addie," Jim said as he stooped down and gently raised Addie up, almost on his own. "Dan's a priest, Congresswoman Perkins is a nurse, and I was an Eagle Scout. Among the three of us, we'll take great care of you."

Addie dropped heavily into a chair, wincing as she moved. "Was it a terrorist attack? Oh, Lord! Look at my little shop!"

"Don't worry about the shop just now," Father Dan tried to soothe her.

Barbara had spent two summers as a student nurse in an Army hospital. Now her triage training kicked in. First, she checked for telltale signs of a head injury, then made sure there was no unusual bleeding, then finally she addressed Addie's shoulder.

"Well, I don't think you've had a concussion. However, you do have a broken arm and probably a dislocated shoulder. Addie, where's the First-Aid kit?"

"It's in back on the right in the storage room," Addie said, attempting to mask her own pain.

"Let me see if I can find some Ace Bandages so I can make you more comfortable. Then we'll clean this mess up."

Barbara made her way to the storage space and returned in a moment, bandages in hand.

"Addie, honey, this is going to hurt, but once I put this bandage on you, you'll feel better." She looked up at Dan. "Now, Father, I need you to hold her arm at right angles, just like that. Mr. Stenson, I need you to gently apply pressure to Addie's shoulder blade. Don't push hard, just gentle pressure. Perfect!" With that, Barbara wrapped Addie's shoulder. "Addie, I want you to take two Extra Strength Tylenol and rest."

"No, not me. I never take anything for pain. I'll be fine, Congress-woman," Addie said without hesitation.

"Addie—I'm more or less ordering you to take these. It may be a while before the ambulance gets here. I'm a Member of Congress—you have to do what I say!" Barbara said with a grin.

Reluctantly, Addie nodded and took the medicine.

As Dan and Barbara turned away, they noticed Bruce slouched by the door.

"Did you call 9-1-1?" Barbara asked sharply.

"I . . . I tried," Bruce struggled with his words, "but there's no cellphone reception. The tunnel isn't passable. It looks like we have no internet connection. It seems the entire tunnel is blocked."

They sat for a moment in silence. The only light came from the refrigerator cases.

"Father Dan," said Addie softly. "Would you please pray for us?"

Hesitantly, Dan nodded, crossed himself, and prayed for Addie that the medicine would reduce her pain, that his four companions would soon be able to resume their day, and that their families would be safe from worry.

"God, please be with those who even now are trying to rescue us. Amen."

When Dan made the sign of the cross and opened his eyes, he saw an unmistakable sneer on Bruce's face.

John McIntyre sat at his desk scribbling notes on his legal pad, trying to compose himself. As Speaker of the House, he knew all too well that within the next five minutes—ten at most—everyone in Washington would be calling him for answers. He needed answers fast. His administrative assistant and most trusted staff person, Lillian Hawkins, had a medical appointment and wouldn't be in until noon.

What an inopportune time for a calamity! John had planned to have the House begin debate on the Department of Defense Appropriations bill at noon. Tomorrow morning, the House Budget Committee would mark up the third concurrent budget resolution. John had sought a number of bipartisan amendments which required—no, demanded—he be present to smooth ruffled feathers. The White House was insisting he come to some brouhaha on technology and the private sector this afternoon. Now all of these plans had ground to a halt after the Speaker spoke to Paul Dupre, Chief of the Capitol Police. John heaved a sigh of relief to hear from the Chief that this was not a terrorist attack.

Now he dialed the Architect of the Capitol.

"Good morning, Ms. Perez."

Simone stopped sipping her coffee and cleared her throat. "G-Good morning, Mr. Speaker," Simone stammered.

"Ms. Perez, I have just spoken to Paul Dupre and I am very relieved to learn this is not an attack. As I understand it, this had to do with the installation of an electrical system in a mechanical room, is that correct? How soon will you have details?"

"That's correct, Mr. Speaker. I am pulling together an interagency committee at 10:00. Both Paul Dupre and Earl Bentsen, Chief of D.C. Fire and Rescue, will be in attendance, as well as Dom Martinelli from our Maintenance Department. I've also asked Pickering Architects, who helped us with renovations last year, to attend. I'm hoping this group can help us understand what happened," Simone said, hoping she sounded cogent.

"Based on what you and the Chief are telling me," said the Speaker, "it seems reasonable to close the Capitol. I must tell you, I'll have a number of unhappy House members since we're starting the Department of Defense Appropriations bill today. But that's certainly not your concern," he hastened to add.

"Closing the Capitol is a good idea for now," Simone replied.

"You obviously have this situation under control. I'll give you my cellphone number. Please keep me up-to-date. One more thing—since you have all the salient details, I'd like you to handle the press. I'll head to the House floor and I'll be in touch soon. If you need me, please call my cellphone." He paused and read out the number to her. "Thanks very much," he said, and hung up.

Simone took a sip of cold coffee and wondered how much more complicated this day would become.

❧

Joel Carlson strode into his tiny office just off the House press gallery and dropped his satchel beside his desk. It made a heavy thud as it hit the floor. To call his desk cluttered would have been a grievous understatement.

Between ancient Congressional Records, empty coffee cups, and half-drafted memos, his actual desk was barely visible. His secretary periodically threatened to make it neat and tidy.

Forget neat and tidy, thought Joel as he skimmed the Associated Press morning report. His desk was just the way he wanted it, and he knew where everything was.

As the House Bureau Chief for *The Washington Post*, Carlson sat at his desk reviewing the amendments cleared last night by the House Rules Committee. Those rules would govern today's consideration of the Department of Defense Appropriations bill. Then, without warning, he heard—and felt—the explosion. Instinctively, he flinched. In his third-floor office he still felt strong vibrations. He wondered if there had been another earthquake like the one in 2011. This felt different somehow.

Almost immediately, a Capitol Police officer ran into the outer office barking, "Okay, everybody, listen up! There's been an explosion and we're evacuating the Capitol. Now! Let's go, please." He was in no mood for conversation.

"What happened, officer?" Joel asked.

"Look, buddy, I've got no idea. All I know is the basement tunnel is partially collapsed, and the Chief's clearing the Dome."

"Okay, but I work for *The Post*, and they're going to want to know"—Joel didn't even finish his sentence.

"Look, pal, that's all I know. Get your stuff and get out, huh?"

Reluctantly, Joel fetched his satchel, turned off his computer, and exited the Capitol. Once outside, he saw several ambulances pull into the House's east portico. Medics and cops were everywhere. Joel knew one thing for certain: this was not a drill.

Quickly, he dialed his boss, Harry Briggs. "So, Harry, something's happened here at the Capitol. The Capitol cops cleared everybody out. Apparently, the tunnel below the Capitol collapsed."

"I'm watching it on CNN," responded Harry. "It's pandemonium. Nobody knows what's going on. It's lucky you've got a front-row seat!"

"Well, I'm thinking you should send one of your desk writers who cover this sort of stuff all the time. I'm sure they'll sound the all-clear any minute now, and the House will gavel in and get to work on Defense Appropriations," Joel said.

"Nothing doing, buddy boy. This is your beat, so this is your baby. You're a competent writer, so let me know how it's going. If they gavel in, you'll figure a way to cover it. My bet is they won't touch that Defense bill today. Stay in touch. Cheers!"

With that, Harry Briggs hung up.

Joel stood on the Capitol steps a moment, gazing at the sea of activity below. He shuddered to think what lay ahead. He sensed this crisis could become bigger than either he or Harry could imagine. With a sigh, he hoisted his satchel up to his shoulder and dialed the Architect of the Capitol with his free hand. Surely, they'd have some answers.

3

JOHN MCINTYRE STRAIGHTENED HIS tie, slipped on his suit coat, and headed for the House floor. After speaking with both the Architect of the Capitol and the Chief of the Capitol Police, it was clear he needed to call the House into recess.

Entering the elevator, he reminded himself to call his eldest daughter and let her know he was fine. His three adult children insisted on hearing from him when something happened on the Hill. He would text Malory as soon as he got off the House floor.

He strode to his desk on the House floor and took the microphone, interrupting Congresswoman Kessler, and began, "I thank the gentlewoman, Ms. Kessler, for yielding the floor to me. Ladies and gentlemen, there was an explosion in the basement of the Capitol just about half an hour ago. The Office of the Architect of the Capitol is gathering information about this incident, especially if there have been any casualties. They will be giving regular news updates throughout the day. We do not believe this is an act of terrorism. Rather, we think the new electrical system somehow exploded. Out of an abundance of caution, I have decided to close the Capitol until further notice. I know that many of you were planning to debate the 2021 Defense Appropriations bill today. Postponing that debate for a day or two is the wisest course of action.

"This is likely to be a very difficult day here in the Capitol. We still don't know the full extent of this tragedy. As this day unfolds, we will make every effort to keep members informed. If you are a person of faith, I ask you pray for the victims of this tragedy as well as those working to rescue them. No matter your religious leanings, please send your good thoughts to the victims as well as those who will rescue them.

"The House stands adjourned, subject to the Call of the Chair. Additionally, I am closing the Capitol to visitors until further notice. Members should check with their respective committee chairs and ranking members, regarding the status of Committee hearings and mark-ups. Thank you very much!"

Thus, the House of Representatives adjourned—indefinitely.

⌒∾

Dom glanced around the conference room quickly as he and Rob entered and took their seats. It astounded him that in just over an hour, Simone Perez had assembled a working group which included representatives from the Capitol Police, D.C. Fire and Rescue Department, and to his chagrin, Vaughn Hanesworth of Pickering Architects.

"Thank you all for coming to this meeting on such short notice," said Simone briskly. "I am Simone Perez, Architect of the Capitol. With us today is Capitol Police Captain Paul Dupre, D.C. Fire and Rescue Chief Earl Bentsen, and Dom Martinelli, Director of Maintenance. I'm also pleased that Vaughn Hanesworth, who is an associate with Pickering Architects, is present. Let me say at the outset that I have been in contact with the Speaker of the House who has asked me to lead the efforts to ascertain what has happened this morning and to keep the press informed about the rescue."

She took a deep breath and continued.

"Let me briefly tell you what I know, and then turn this meeting over to Captain Dupre and Chief Bentsen. At approximately 8:36 a.m., a massive explosion occurred in the basement of the Capitol. We do not believe this is a terrorist attack. Rather, we believe this explosion is the result of the installation of a new electrical system. We have evacuated eighteen people thus far who have non-life-threatening injuries. Tourists comprise the majority of evacuees; although several Hill staffers are also in transit to the hospital with minor injuries. We anticipate there will be more injured persons throughout the day. Now, I'd like to ask Captain Dupre to give us an update."

Captain Dupre stood and looked around at the group. "Well, as you mentioned, Ms. Perez, we believe this explosion is the direct result of the installation of a new digital electrical system, although we won't be able to confirm this until we're able to reach the mechanical room. As Mr. Martinelli will explain further, the underground tunnel has almost entirely collapsed. Because these tunnels are impassable right now, and we are not certain of the structural integrity of the Capitol, I've spoken to the Speaker of the House and he has closed the Capitol until further notice. That's all I have at the moment. I'd ask my colleague at the District of Columbia Fire and Rescue Department, Chief Earl Bentsen to say a few words."

Earl smiled and said, "Thanks Paul. As most of you know, the D.C. Fire and Rescue Department comes to the Hill fairly infrequently. It therefore surprised me when we received a three-alarm fire call at approximately 8:46 this morning, requesting both fire and ambulance assistance. I've spoken to my staff and we have sent four ambulances to Washington Hospital Center. What bothers me most, frankly, is what we do not know. We do not definitively know the cause of this explosion, although the cutover of the new electrical system is certainly a plausible explanation. Has the structural integrity of the tunnels been compromised? Most important, we do not know if there are people trapped in all this mess, and if so, how we can get to them. From where I am, it looks like a long day ahead.

"I'm wondering if we could use FINDER, which is an acronym for Finding Individuals for Disaster and Emergency Response. The NSA developed this technology and it allows us to detect human heartbeats and therefore find trapped victims. Homeland Security has used this technology successfully, as have many others. I'd feel much better if I knew where the victims are."

Dom spoke up. "Chief, I've heard about this technology in the past. My staff will do some research. I'll have an update for you at the next meeting." He glanced at his secretary, Stella, who gave him a nod and murmured, "I'm on it, Boss."

Simone thanked him and said, "I'd now like to turn this meeting over to Dom Martinelli. For those of you who don't know, Dom has served with distinction as the Director of Maintenance for thirty-six years. Dom, please tell us what you know about the cutover of the new electrical system, and what you are doing."

Dom cleared his throat, momentarily taken aback by Simone's flattering comments. "Here's what we know: the explosion took place in the mechanical room in the basement of the Capitol on the House side. We are replacing the old electrical system with a new one in order to support a process called cogeneration. Cogeneration combines heat and power in order to conserve energy. My staff is also looking for the schematic drawings of the tunnel which should help with the search-and-rescue operations. Now I would ask Mr. Rob Tate to speak. Rob has been involved with the installation of the new electrical system and has found what may be our best hope of finding any survivors."

Rob said a silent prayer for help and stood. He noticed an easel with some felt-tipped markers at the other end of the table. He moved around to the easel and said, "Let me draw you a picture of what I know. Right after the explosion, I went down and tried to go through the tunnel on the House side. As Ms. Perez said, there's nothing but a wall of rubble. Think of the tunnel as a large arch—with a couple of quirky turns." As he drew, he tried to make eye contact.

"Go on," Simone said.

"When I went to the Senate side of the tunnel, I could walk in maybe fifteen feet. At one of those turns there's a meat locker which refrigerates food for a number of eating venues throughout the Capitol. Next to this unit there's a vent space about fifteen feet up. I was able to get into this space and proceed about thirty-five feet further into the tunnel. My goal is to keep going further into this vent space until I reach the mechanical room. Then we can figure out more of what's going on."

"How wide is this vent space?" Simone interrupted. "I ask because if it's big enough we might be able to get some supplies and equipment through."

Rob shook his head. "To be honest, I'm a skinny guy, but I can just barely get through walking on my elbows. So, I'm not sure if we can get any equipment through."

Chief Bentsen leaned forward. "We've got some audio equipment that's very small. Actually, it's much like the bugging devices you see on these TV cop shows. If we could attach one of these to you, we might be able to figure out where the survivors are. It could complement our work with the FINDER system."

Dom added, "My department has some Bobcat devices they use when they're searching for survivors after bombings. It allows guys to clear the rubble—but they've also got sensors to detect human life so we can rescue survivors."

Simone cleared her throat. "Dom, obviously you have a clear understanding of what needs to be done. I have a few more questions for Rob." She turned to him. "How far do you think this vent space goes? Could you show us on your drawing where the mechanical room is, and any other points where there might be survivors?"

Rob thought for a moment, then said, "If you enter the tunnel from the Senate side, there's a carpenter's shop on the left-hand side." He drew a small box. "Down about thirty feet from that, on the right-hand side, is a small coffee shop." He marked the spot with a large X. "That would have been full about the time of the blast. Then, about twenty feet further down the tunnel, there's a small alcove leading to the mechanical room." He drew an arrow leading to the mechanical room and capped the marker. "Does that make sense?" he asked.

Dom stood. "If we think about this tunnel, it's really important to remember the Capitol is an historic structure and it's got layers and layers which have been added over time. The vent space Rob's struggling through is over one hundred twenty-five years old. I mention this because it's the layers of this building that are going to add to the complexity of this rescue."

Vaughn Hanesworth interrupted. "As most of you know, Pickering Architects specializes in the historic aspects of the Capitol. It is a complex structure, as Mr. Martinelli just explained in a rather rudimentary fashion. Before we continue any further, Ms. Perez, I must strenuously object to this young man crawling around in this so-called vent space. This could do irreparable damage to this vent space which—if my memory serves me— dates back to the 1850s. I would think you'd share this concern."

"I will take your concerns under advisement," Simone said. "Right now, I am solely concerned about rescuing survivors, thank you."

"You'll regret that decision, I can assure you," Vaughn snapped.

Simone's face tightened briefly as she turned back to Rob. "I have a couple more questions, if you don't mind. Are you wearing a protective mask? Also, forgive me Dom, but I must insist that Mr. Tate only be in that space for forty-five minutes per hour."

"Ms. Perez!" Rob pleaded. "Look, ma'am, with all due respect, that's not enough time. I'll be fine, really."

"I very much appreciate your dedication to finding survivors," Simone replied. "Nevertheless, you'll do us no good if you become exhausted. Besides, since you're the only one with expertise to help us, we'll need you at these update meetings throughout the day and likely well into the evening."

Rob opened his mouth to respond, but felt Dom's massive hand on his shoulder. "We'll take good care of him, Ms. Perez. Don't you worry."

Simone nodded and smiled, then continued. "I have a few more items. Mr. Hanesworth, how soon will Pickering be able to put together a team of engineers to help us assess the building's structural integrity? The Speaker of the House has closed the Capitol for the time being. I know he's very anxious to get this task completed as soon as possible."

"The engineering team will assemble within the hour. We cannot rush this important process," Vaughn responded.

"I am very aware of that. Just keep me apprised of your progress," Simone said, glancing at him. "My staff will be compiling a list of injured or deceased."

Her staff exchanged glances.

"The press is everywhere," Simone continued. "I will hold a press conference right after this meeting. Captain Dupre and Chief Bentsen, I'd be grateful if you could join me. Dom, I'd like you there as well. I'll do most of the talking, but it'd be helpful to have your expertise available. Its 11:15 now: Let's meet here again at 1:00 p.m. My office will provide lunch. Thanks everybody!"

She stood up and gathered her papers as the meeting broke up, each person leaving with an assignment.

Despite most of the rubble in the coffee shop now being cleaned up, and the tables and chairs put back in place, it was obvious their rescue would not be happening soon. With Bruce's help, Dan had managed to set up a make-shift privy. Addie's pain seemed better, but she still needed medical attention. Bruce's wrist had swollen to the size of a golf ball. Dan told everyone he felt fine, yet his headache was merciless.

"Wow, thanks for cleaning up guys," said Barbara. "It really helps to be able to move around! Addie, honey, you should eat something. Actually, we should all eat a snack. At least we have food. Plus, we have an endless supply of caffeine options!"

"Well," Addie responded hesitantly, "I'd love a bagel. But I don't know if I should eat since I'm a diabetic and I don't really know when my next insulin shot will be."

Dan couldn't help but notice the look of concern that flashed across Barbara's face. "When did you take your last dose, Addie?"

She sat silent for a moment. "Well, see, I've been sorta cutting back. That insulin costs a small fortune. I have my grandsons to think about . . ." Addie looked like a small child caught being naughty.

"Okay, Miss Addie. When did you take your last dose?" Barbara insisted.

"Yesterday, at about 4:30. You see, I take it and then go fix supper. We eat at 5:30, because I want my boys to digest their food before bedtime."

"Addie, I want you to eat this turkey and drink some juice. Then you can have half a bagel. I'll eat the other half," said Barbara, handing her the food.

Addie appeared famished, but before she would eat, she bowed her head and quietly said, "Thank you, Lord, for this food I'm about to eat. May it nourish my body and my soul. Please bless these kind folks who are here with me. I pray most especially for Mr. Bruce. Lord, he has a big hearing today and lots of work, so please help him. Finally, bless those who are coming to get us. In Jesus's name, Amen."

"Amen," echoed Dan as he unwrapped one of the sandwiches from the refrigerator case.

"One more thing, y'all. Please list what you're eatin', but you can pay later." Addie was still in charge.

Jim laughed and said, "Addie, I'm glad to pay for what I eat. Considering the fact our entire workday is probably shot and we all have some battle scars, I'm guessing this lunch is on Uncle Sam."

Barbara walked over and placed two Tylenol in front of Bruce. "Your wrist is clearly broken, young man. Take these with your sandwich. It'll ease the pain a bit. In a minute, I'll go back to the first aid supplies and find an Ace Bandage for your wrist."

Bruce looked up, befuddled. "Thanks very much, Congresswoman."

"Look, I'm Barbara. Forget politics for today. This is just something we'll have to help each other through."

"Yes, I guess so." Bruce swallowed the pills and washed them down with a Coke.

Gradually, the occupants of the café broke off into groups, some in quiet conversation. Still, two occupants held back. Bruce was lost in thought about the hearing he would miss, while Dan sat staring into space, his head throbbing, wondering why he could not find the courage to minister to this tiny flock.

❧

At 11:20, the phone rang. Colleen answered, expecting yet another telemarketer.

"Good morning, is Mrs. Larson there? This is Sue Darden with Congressman John Chamberlin's office."

"Yes, this is Colleen Larson," she answered.

"Is Father Larson sick or something? I'm Congressman Chamberlin's appointments secretary and it's very unusual for Father to miss the regular monthly meetings."

"Sue," said Colleen anxiously, "my husband left for his meeting with the Congressman at 7:15 this morning. He always goes in early so he's not tardy to the meeting. Usually he stops for coffee and . . ."

All at once tears sprang to Colleen's eyes.

"Do you think my husband was caught in the explosion at the Capitol this morning? I mean, surely they've gotten everyone out by now, haven't they?" She was finding it difficult to breathe.

Sue was silent for a moment. "Mrs. Larson, let me look into this further. I'm sure there's an explanation. If you should hear from him, please call me right away. I will call you back within the hour. And please, take my personal number."

Colleen hung up the receiver and stared blankly at the phone.

❧

Chief Bentsen suited up and headed toward the tunnel. He'd learned a great deal from the interagency meeting, but now he needed to assess the situation for himself. As he put his helmet on, he noticed EMT Paula Winthrop checking the supplies in her ambulance.

"Paula!" he called out. "How's business? Have you taken any additional folks to the hospital? I've been in a meeting with muckety-mucks."

"Chief, it's been really quiet. Too quiet, if you catch my drift." Paula flashed him a look.

"I do," he responded. "If things are quiet, walk with me. I could use some feedback. Besides, I can brag about my grandbaby's first piano recital," Earl chuckled.

"Sure! Let me get my gear and I'll join you." Paula told her colleagues where she and the Chief were heading, and soon the two were walking together toward the tunnel.

Earl Bentsen's affable demeanor made him easy to talk to. Rookies sometimes thought he appeared to be a nice guy who knew little or nothing about the fire and rescue business. Those who made such an assessment were mistaken. Beneath his easy smile and gentle ways were nerves of steel. Earl Bentsen had seen it all. Like every little boy, he had wanted to grow up to be a fireman—and he had never outgrown that longing. As a young boy, he had hung out at the local fire station, and when a call came in he begged to ride along. He always wanted to know the details of how a fire started. Did they have enough hands to put the fire out? Was the family okay? Could they save the home? Earl never stopped learning. Folks who were lucky enough to work for the Chief learned from him daily.

Paula broke the silence. "So, Chief, how bad is it?"

He walked a few more paces, considering her question. Then he said, "Well, Paula, I'm glad this isn't a terrorist attack. That's everyone's worst nightmare. However, I'm concerned about what we don't know. There were two guys in the mechanical room: Are they still alive? We think there are probably some survivors, but we don't know where they are. At this point, there are more questions than answers. I am encouraged by one thing I learned in my meeting. There's a young man, Rob Tate, with the Maintenance Department. He's a skinny fellow who's managed to get into a vent space above the collapsed tunnel. We hope he can somehow climb through the vent space to the mechanical room and assess the situation."

The Chief and Paula were in the tunnel now, seeing the utter destruction of the entire House side of the tunnel. The Chief spoke to some of the maintenance crew working to clear the rubble from the space. It would be slow going.

"Let's walk over to the Senate side," Bentsen said. "I want to see as much as I can in the next thirty minutes."

They took the elevator to the first floor and walked through Statuary Hall, eerily quiet now. Normally, this space would be bustling with staffers and tourists, members of Congress and dignitaries, all seeking to understand and perhaps influence American democracy. The Chief led the way down a secluded hallway to a small elevator which took them to the basement floor. After a few unlikely turns, Chief Bentsen and Paula found themselves face-to-face with a huge meat locker. Just across the hall, Rob Tate and Dom Martinelli were in an animated discussion. The Chief spoke first.

"You fellas hear anything yet? By the way, I'd like both of you to meet EMT Paula Winthrop. Paula and I are making the rounds. How's it going here?"

Dom smiled and said, "Paula, this is Rob Tate. He works with me in Capitol Maintenance. He hopes to get through that vent space to the mechanical room."

"Is there anything I can do to help?" Paula asked.

"Not now, but maybe later," Dom said. Then he turned to the Chief and asked, "What's your honest assessment of this situation?"

"I'll need a few more hours before I can really answer that question. The work you two are doing may help us figure out exactly what we need to do," Earl said. He continued, "Once we know if there are any victims alive, then we can better figure out a rescue plan. It's going to take a few more hours of everyone doing their jobs. Paula and I will be on our way. I'll see you gentlemen at the 1:00 meeting. Stay safe, Rob."

As they walked back to the staging area outside of the Capitol, Earl said, "Paula, I want you to consider helping Rob in the vent space. You're a petite woman, and chances are there will be some victims who really may need your care. I'm not asking for a commitment now—just think about it. Let's see where things stand after the next interagency meeting."

"Chief, I'll be glad to help," Paula said. "You just say the word."

They walked for a while in silence until Paula looked up at the Chief with a grin and asked, "So, tell me about this piano recital."

Earl Bentsen's face brightened with a broad smile as he described his six year-old granddaughter's piano recital in great detail. Chuckling, he said, "Paula, she looked so serious. There she is in her pink frilly dress, and her feet didn't even touch the pedals. There she sat playing, 'Row, Row, Row Your Boat,' but you'd think she was playing Mozart in Carnegie Hall. That baby looked so funny."

They laughed as they walked, both considering how and when a rescue could take place.

❧

Rob Tate struggled to put on all the new gear he needed in order to get back up into the vent space. Between his hard hat, the now-required mask, a new bugging device, and his safety harness, he felt encumbered and bulky—like a small child going out to play in a snow suit.

Dom bent over and adjusted Rob's harness. "Okay," he said. "All you need to do is keep this button on and the transmitter will pick up any sounds. If you want to talk to someone in the tunnel push 'broadcast' and it becomes a megaphone." Dom looked at Rob intently. "I want you to be as comfortable as possible. If you want to tell me something, just push this button. It works just like an intercom system."

"Thanks, Dom. Well, here goes." Rob flashed him a thumbs-up and clambered up the ladder into the vent space. He flicked on his hard-hat light, grateful for its focused, white beam. Slowly, he squirmed forward through the narrow space, listening for any sounds.

He wiggled through the cramped space to the first of three turns. As he tried to negotiate in the tight space, he realized the turn narrowed the vent space even further. He paused for a moment, uncertain if he'd be able to make the next turn.

"Hey, Dom, I may be in a jam," Rob said into his walkie-talkie. "This turn is much tighter than I thought, but I really want to keep going."

"Rob, you'll be fine," Dom's voice crackled in the vent. "I've got the other end of the harness. The wife says I'm strong as an ox. If you get stuck, I'll get you back. Just keep talking to me,"

"Copy that," Rob muttered.

With all the strength he could muster, he squirmed his way around the turn and breathed a sigh of relief as he slid through.

"Dom, I'm through and I've got some good news. It looks like there's a perpendicular intersection about twenty-five feet ahead. I'm going to broadcast and try to at least make the T turn before we need to go to the meeting."

"Okay, Rob. Good job. We have about twenty minutes until the next conference.

Rob hit the "broadcast" button and called out, "Anybody there?" He paused and listened, but heard nothing. He called out again and waited. He had almost turned around when he heard a series of distinct clanks on pipes somewhere. He held his breath and listened. "Dom, did you hear that?"

"Roger that! I think it could be Morse code for SOS. We'll be back within the hour. I'll urge Simone to excuse us so we can get you back up there."

Rob sighed. "I just hate to leave, knowing someone's asking for help," he said.

Dom grinned to himself. "Yeah, I know. However, if you're going to help them, you need to stay strong. Let's get to this meeting, eat ourselves silly, and then maybe you can stay up longer," Dom said.

"Hey, Dom, do me a favor. Ask Stella to bring me a fresh shirt."

Rob Tate made his way out of the vent space wondering who sent the SOS.

4

SIMONE STEPPED UP TO the podium.

"Good morning, ladies and gentlemen. If you would kindly take your seats, we can get started. My name is Simone Perez, and I am the Architect of the Capitol. The Speaker of the House has asked me to brief you on the events of this morning.

"At eight thirty-six this morning, an explosion took place in one of the underground tunnels which connect the Senate to the House of Representatives. We are early in our investigation, but let me tell you what we know, and then we can discuss what we don't know.

"We know for certain that terrorists did not attack us. Rather, we believe this explosion is the result of the installation of a new electrical system. At this point we are working very hard to determine if there are any fatalities and, of course, to get the injured to the hospital.

"We have put together an interagency task force to look at how best to proceed. Represented on that task force are Captain Paul Dupre, Chief of the Capitol Police; Earl Bentsen, Chief of the D.C. Fire and Rescue Department; and Dom Martinelli, who heads the Capitol Maintenance Department. This team will be working around the clock to rescue any survivors.

"Out of an abundance of caution, the Speaker has closed the Capitol so we can get to any survivors, and in order to ascertain the structural integrity of the Capitol itself. Representatives of Pickering Architects, led by Vaughn Hanesworth, will be helping us make this determination. Some of you may know that Mr. Hanesworth recently helped with some of the renovations to the dome.

"I will now take a few questions," Simone finished, pointing to one of the reporters.

Kyle Brown with *USA Today* asked, "Ms. Perez, you said this is not a terrorist attack, yet in the very next breath you stated, 'We believe that this is the result of the installation of a new electrical system.' Isn't it the case that you do not know for certain what exactly caused the explosion and you won't know for a while?"

"Mr. Brown, I do not agree with your assessment," said Simone, shaking her head. "Our new electrical system awaits inspection by the Capitol Power Plant. This is where the initial explosion took place. To speculate otherwise would be to send all of us on a fool's errand.

"Ms. Payne with the *New York Times*," said Simone.

"Ms. Perez, do you know how long the Capitol will be closed? And as a follow-up: Do you know how long the tunnel which connects the Senate and the House will be shut down?"

"Ms. Payne, we have a small army of engineers evaluating the structural viability of the Capitol. Pickering Architects is leading this effort. It's not clear how long their evaluation may take."

She pointed again, "Finally, Ms. Redden with *Politico*."

"Ms. Perez, several key hearings were scheduled to take place in the Capitol today. Will new hearing rooms be found, and if so, by whom? And what about the DOD bill?"

"My office is working on this issue. Some hearings have already been reassigned new rooms. I would ask for your patience as we scramble to meet these demands under extenuating circumstances. The House had been scheduled to debate the Department of Defense appropriations bill today. It is my understanding this will be debated as soon as it's safe for the House to meet.

"That's it for now. We'll brief you again this afternoon at five-thirty. Thanks everybody," said Simone. She gathered up her papers and stepped away from the podium.

Fred opened his eyes slowly. Nothing looked right and he couldn't figure out where he was. He called out to his wife, desperately seeking her comfort. A sharp, acrid odor burned in his nostrils. His ears rang and his eyes burned from blue smoke which hung in the room. Suddenly, he realized the horror of the explosion. Fred coughed and rubbed his eyes and called out, "Billy! Talk to me, man! Are you there?"

For several long moments he heard nothing. Then he heard a low moan from nearby. Fred strained to sit up, trying to see through the haze.

Finally, he heard a low raspy whisper: Billy muttering, "I'm here, brother. I'm hurt real bad."

I've got to get to him, Fred thought.

His head throbbed and his vision blurred. He tried to stand, but he couldn't push away the debris that pinned him up against a wall. He closed his eyes and lay back, exhausted, tried to think. No matter how he tried to get his thoughts in the right order, they drifted away like smoke. He struggled again to sit up, but his body seemed to be floating.

I've got to stay awake, he thought, just before the blackness rose behind his eyes and he sank back into unconsciousness.

~

"Yes, Senator Hobbs, I share your concerns about the structural integrity of the Capitol. A team of engineers is assessing this as we speak. I promise I will get back to you on this matter as soon as we receive definitive information. Thanks for understanding." Simone Perez hung up the phone and sighed heavily.

She'd somehow managed to keep up with the myriad of Congressional phone calls that were coming in. It was becoming painfully obvious this crisis would not be over soon. She had just picked up the phone to return yet another call when a knock on her door interrupted her thoughts. She looked up to see John McIntyre, Speaker of the House, smiling at her. "Excuse me, Ms. Perez. I need a word with you. May I come in?"

Instinctively, Simone stood up and responded, "Certainly. Please come in, Mr. Speaker."

The Speaker quickly motioned for her to sit, and she relaxed a little.

"First of all, I stopped by to thank you for skillfully handling the press. You did a fine job."

"Thank you, sir," Simone said as she glanced at her notes and shuffled them without thinking. She tried to focus, desperately seeking to compose herself.

He leaned forward. "Can you tell me how soon we will know when it will be safe to use the House Chamber? I ask because we were supposed to begin debating the DOD Appropriations bill today. Some members are concerned we're losing valuable debate time."

"Mr. Speaker, that's difficult to say." She looked away for a moment and then back at him. "It's my understanding that Vaughn Hanesworth with Pickering Architects is using a team of structural engineers to look at this problem as we speak. I'm hoping they can give you an answer by days end. Obviously, working hand-in-glove with the D.C. Fire and Rescue Department Chief Bentsen is particularly helpful," Simone said.

"Excellent!" John exclaimed. "That will help me with my colleagues who are so eager to do the people's business." He stood to leave, but noticed a series of photographs neatly arranged on the wall. "I must ask—these buildings"—he waved a hand at the wall—"What's the background behind these photographs? They're beautiful!"

"Well, thank you, Mr. Speaker," Simone smiled. "Actually, they are buildings I designed at various points in my career. Two are in Seattle, two are in New Orleans, and one is in Portland. They are like old friends. Sometimes it's easy to forget where you've been."

She smiled, noticing the Speaker's jaunty appearance, despite his graying hair.

"Getting back to the business at hand," the Speaker said. "Tell me something: when you consider what may have happened in the tunnel, what are you most concerned about?" He paused briefly, smiling. "Before you answer, my name is not 'Mr. Speaker.' It's John. Please, let's dispense with the formalities, shall we?" he chuckled.

"Sure, but I'm Simone, okay? You asked what I'm most concerned about. That's easy: I'm scared that people are hurt, and that there may be loss of life. I know this is irrational, but I feel somehow responsible. I'm especially concerned about those who may be in the café. Addie Hutchison is a friend of mine . . ." Simone's voice trailed off.

"Simone, I doubt there's anything either of us could have done to prevent this. I know how you feel. I hope and pray there's no loss of life. I have to contend with all the members of the House, many of whom have significant legislative agendas, and most of whom are upset with me for giving them the day off. House consideration of DOD appropriations is postponed. My members were really looking forward to, shall we say, 'vigorous debate.' In other words, the Democrats plan to stick it to the Republicans and vice versa," John said.

"I'll keep you up to date on any developments, John. Of course, I'll alert you if we learn of fatalities." Simone looked down.

John rose to leave but a small photograph on Simone's credenza caught his eye. The picture captured Simone intently playing the cello in an orchestra. "Is that you playing the cello? You look very intense!"

Simone smiled. "Yes, I've played the cello since I was nine. It's an avocation for me. In that picture, I'm playing with the Seattle Community

Philharmonic Orchestra. A little orchestra comprised of a few doctors, lawyers, plus a few stay-at-home moms. As for my intense look, we were playing Brahms's 'Requiem,' which is a rather tough piece. I really loved playing with that group."

"Perhaps I can hear you play sometime," John said.

"Perhaps," Simone said, suddenly embarrassed she'd volunteered such personal information.

"I'll be in touch after lunch. Call me if something comes up."

With that, the Speaker of the House left.

❧

Colleen Larson hurriedly pulled herself together in a pair of dress jeans and turtleneck sweater. She kept the radio on WTOP, a station noted for news in the Washington area, hoping to hear the collapse of the tunnel on Capitol Hill had been resolved and her husband would be home soon. Instead she heard:

"I'm reporting live from Capitol Hill and this is what we know at the moment. The collapse of the tunnel has sent twenty people to the hospital so far—most of those were staff or tourists . . ."

Colleen flipped the radio off, annoyed at the dearth of information about the explosion. She was having trouble breathing and her thoughts were jumbled and erratic. She kept asking herself, *What should I do?*

She'd been a pastor's wife for twenty-seven years—but at the moment all she could muster was two words, "Please God."

Her cellphone rang, "Hello, this is Colleen Larson."

"Mom, what's up with the formal greeting? Are you expecting the Queen of England?" Amy Larson joked.

"Honey; look," said Colleen, choking back tears, "I need to talk to you. There's been an accident in one of the tunnels on Capitol Hill. Daddy always stops for coffee at the shop in the tunnel and I haven't heard from him since he left this morning. I don't know what to do. Congressman Chamberlin's office called me an hour ago. Daddy didn't show up for his meeting and they wondered if he was sick or something. You want to know what's really nuts. All I can pray is 'Please God.' Amy, honey, I really need you!"

"Mom, I'm on my way home! I should be there in twenty minutes. Text me if you hear anything—anything at all."

❧

Amy hung up and then texted two of her professors concerning her absence. Then she ran as fast as she could to her car, echoing her mother's prayer, "Please God."

∾

Joel walked for blocks, lost in thought. He had to get back to work, yet he was numb with shock. When he called Barbara Perkins's office to chat, she wasn't there. Her staff hoped Joel would have some explanation. There was no answer from her cellphone, and Barbara was gone before her housekeeper arrived that morning. It seemed pretty clear Barbara was likely a casualty of the explosion in the Capitol. Twenty minutes ago, this was just another story Joel was writing for *The Washington Post*. Now it was a deeply personal matter: it was a story that most probably involved the love of his life.

Still, he had to smile when he thought back to six months ago. They had met by chance at—of all things—a lecture on a Sunday afternoon at the Library of Congress. They had recognized each other from a story he'd done on one of her legislative efforts. They sat together for the lecture, and afterwards he'd asked her to go with him for drinks at the Hawk and Dove. Drinks became dinner and they talked about everything. They had a common love for the outdoors, were avid readers, and both loved folk music.

He fondly remembered the first time he took her for a long ride on his Harley Davidson through the Shenandoah Valley. He could still feel her arms firmly around his mid-section as they drove along. He remembered well the first kiss that he stole that day. His feelings for her had grown stronger over the last several months. Although they spent most weekends camping or traveling, he always sensed she was holding back. Except for a few late dinners during the work week, they never saw each other until Friday afternoons. On weekends, he threw a couple pairs of jeans in a duffle bag and headed for her house. What began as simply drinks after a lecture had turned into a tenderness neither of them had ever known.

He ducked into a Starbucks and ordered a grande mocha, then sat down and finished a draft. Joel checked his facts then filed a hastily written, yet accurate, article. The cadence of the article lagged in parts.

Ah well, he thought, *this is the best* The Washington Post *is going to get out of this old boy today.*

He emailed the article to his boss, Harry, grabbed his satchel and his coffee, and headed back up to the Hill to find any information he could about Barbara.

5

"EZRA, PLEASE LISTEN TO me for a moment." The Speaker took a deep breath and shifted the phone to his other hand. Congressman Ezra Martin, a Democrat from St. Louis, had been his good friend for many years. "I fully understand your position on the Civil Rights Commission nominees! Frankly, the Administration sent up some real stooges this time. I give you my solemn word I'll correct this. Right now, I'm worried about the tunnel explosion. Lives may be lost."

John leaned forward as he listened to his friend's complaints. Everything Ezra said was absolutely true: Out of four people which the Administration had nominated to serve on the prestigious Civil Rights Commission, only one had any legal experience and the others had very dubious credentials.

"Listen, I have lunch with the Minority Leader in five minutes to discuss the DOD appropriations bill, and with the Capitol closed, everybody and their mother's uncle has questions. I'll be coming over to the Ways and Means meeting later this afternoon. Let's talk more after that."

As John hung up the phone, his secretary, Lillian Hawkins, came in with a fistful of messages to return. She stood in front of his desk awaiting his instructions. John quickly flipped through his messages, his reading glasses perched precariously on his nose.

"Mrs. Hawkins, you should have gone home after your appointment this morning. The Capitol is closed, you know."

"Mr. Speaker, you know as well as I do that I am safe. My job is to make certain that you have what you need. So, tell me which of those calls I can take care of, then you'd better get a move on, sir. I made your reservations at the House Dining Room with the Minority Leader for 12:30." Lillian looked at her watch then added, "You're already eight minutes late."

Lillian had worked for John from the very beginning of his political career. Petite and well-dressed, she always kept the Speaker focused and on schedule. He'd hired the young African-American woman right out of secretarial school and she'd been at his side through thick and thin. Lillian offered him the mooring he desperately needed.

"Lillian, call this woman at the White House and explain that because of the explosion this morning, I am unable to attend the Technology Symposium. Also, tell Congressman Jacobs to call the Architect of the Capitol. She'll arrange for hearing space. Oh, and Lillian, please call my daughter Julie and tell her I'm fine." John reached for his suit coat and adjusted his tie. Then he casually asked, "Lillian, do you happen to know Simone Perez? What's your impression of her?"

Lillian took the messages and looked at him quizzically. "I've heard she's very bright."

He winked and said, "After lunch, I'm headed for the Ways and Means Committee meeting in the Rayburn Building. Then I'm going to an Interagency meeting that Ms. Perez set up on the explosion. I have my phone on should anything come up."

Lillian nodded as he hurried out the door and called after him, "Mr. Speaker, the Congressional Budget Office plans to send over a couple of guys to review language for the DOD Appropriations bill. I told them to be here at 4:30 sharp."

"Thanks, Lillian!" the Speaker called over his shoulder as he sprinted for the elevator.

∿

"Okay, everyone, please get a plate of food and take your seats. We have a lot of ground to cover this afternoon," said Simone as she began the meeting. "Dom, please tell us what you and Rob have found out so far. Specifically, what can you tell us about the removal of debris from the tunnel? And then, please tell us what progress Rob is making in reaching the mechanical room."

Dom thought for a moment and then said, "I've pulled all of our maintenance personnel and divided them into two teams. They're working at opposite ends of the tunnel and will meet in the middle. They're working slowly so they don't miss anything. So far, they've discovered two people within the rubble. Thanks to D.C. Fire and Rescue, both of these individuals were transported to Washington Hospital Center."

As Dom talked, Vaughn Hanesworth entered the conference room, took two sandwiches, and noisily found a seat.

Dom continued. "I've asked the teams to plan on working 'round the clock. I am hoping this will go faster than we expected. Now I'll turn the meeting over to Rob Tate."

Simone turned to Rob. "Mr. Tate, how goes it in the vent space?"

"Well, I was able to get considerably farther into the space than I did the first time," Rob said, moving to the flip chart he had used earlier that morning. "We heard what sounded like an SOS call further down in the tunnel." He marked the spot on his drawing. "I believe it's coming from the coffee shop. But I won't know until I get further down the vent space."

Chief Bentsen asked, "Any idea how many people may be in the café? Dom, assuming there are victims trapped in the café, how can we reach them? I don't want to jump to conclusions, but this is the type of information we'll need sooner rather than later."

Dom paused and then said, "That's a difficult question to answer at this point, since the only way to get to the café would be through the tunnels. Of course, we're working to determine the structural integrity of the tunnel as we speak."

Dom looked over at Vaughn Hanesworth, who cleared his throat and said, "Yes, well, as Ms. Perez is already aware, the engineers from Pickering are currently working on assessing the viability of the Capitol Building itself." He put down his sandwich. "This assessment includes both the House and Senate chambers. Then, and only then, can our engineers turn their attention to the structural integrity of the tunnel."

Earl Bentsen spoke up. "Vaughn, how many projects have you and I worked on over the years, do you think? I'm guessing at least eight."

Vaughn looked up and said, "We've worked on numerous projects over the years. You have always respected my opinions about the importance of historic preservation of the many critical Federal structures in this city."

"That is exactly my point," Earl continued. "In this particular instance I simply cannot abide by your wishes. We cannot wait until Pickering's engineers are good and ready before we get into that tunnel. Allow me to give you a few facts. Within one hour after an incident like this—one hour—victims can begin to lose critical life functions. The more time it takes to find our victims, the higher the likelihood of permanent disabilities or fatalities. Lives are at stake and I won't sit by and watch."

Turning to Simone, Earl said, "Ms. Perez, I am reluctant to tell you how to do your job. Nevertheless, I think we should get some additional engineers in here as soon as possible. They can do an initial assessment and the Pickering fellas can sign off. Whatever the process, we need extra engineers immediately."

Simone tapped her pencil on the desk, considering her options, then said, "Actually, I have the authority to hire extra personnel as I see fit during emergency situations." She raised a hand as Vaughn cleared his throat. "Vaughn, please hear me out before you respond. What if I hire five extra engineers just to assist us with assessment of the tunnel's structural viability?" Vaughn rose to object, but Simone again put up her hand to silence him and continued, "If we agree to this, I will personally supervise these contractors and make it very clear that if they encounter anything remotely affecting the historic nature of the tunnel, they will stop their work immediately and consult with you. That allows Pickering to focus on its area of expertise while we use the extra engineers to more quickly assess the integrity of the tunnel."

Earl smiled broadly and said, "Now that makes a lot more sense! Since we already know the tunnel has sustained serious damage, the extra personnel should help us find the victims quicker."

Vaughn let out a heavy sigh and leaned back in his chair, both hands on his substantial girth. His mouth was set in a hard line, like a chess player plotting his next move. Although he disdained the idea of bringing in extra engineers as contractors, even he had to admit it made some sense. "Ms. Perez, given where we find ourselves, I suppose you have no choice. Still, I must warn all of you to be mindful of any and all historic portions of the tunnel. It would be helpful if we could establish some sort of communication system so that you could alert the Pickering staff if you encounter a problem."

Before Simone could respond, Dom Martinelli spoke up, "We have high-powered walkie-talkies. I'll have Stella bring them to you after this meeting. I agree that if Vaughn's team is, say, in the Senate chamber, it's crucial that we be able to chat back and forth."

"Super!" Simone exclaimed. "Vaughn, we'll stay in constant contact with you. I give you my word."

Turning back to Rob, Simone asked, "How bad is the vent space? Is it safe? Do we need to find reinforcements?"

Rob shook his head. "I don't think reinforcements are necessary. It's very dusty up there, but it's bearable. I appreciate the offer, but my concern is that someone new won't know the building like I do and would just slow down the recovery effort considerably."

The meeting dragged on, with discussion of press strategies, how to keep members of Congress apprised of their progress, and how they should notify the families of the victims. There was never a good time for Rob and Dom to break away.

Finally, Simone exclaimed, "Okay, this has been a productive meeting. It's 1:50 now. Let's reconvene at 4:30. If I need to speak with anyone, I'll contact you directly."

With that, the meeting concluded.

❧

Makayla Wainwright arrived at roll call early. She was a widely respected veteran of the Capitol Police with a sense of humor. On more than one occasion everyone cracked up with an offhanded comment she made during roll call. Her secret weapon was everyone loved her.

Makayla walked into Captain Dupre's office. "Sir, please, I need a word with you."

"Makayla, this is a terrible day. Please, can this wait?" asked the Captain.

"Sir, do you know Addie Hutchison? She runs the coffee shop in the tunnel."

"I don't know if she's okay," interrupted the Captain.

"Sir, I know that and I know how stressful this must be on you. Here's the thing: Addie's raising three grandkids by herself. I go to her church and I know there's nobody to check on those kids. Frankly, Addie's neighbors, well, they're not exactly family folks if you know what I mean." Makayla's huge brown eyes looked up at him, pleadingly.

Captain Dupre heaved a weary sigh. This was a lousy day and he couldn't afford to let one of his best officers take the whole day babysitting. Still, the Capitol Police force recognized Addie Hutchison as one of their own. "I know what you want, Makayla. Okay, look, after roll call you and Davis go down to Addie's house and fetch the boys. Bring them back here to the office. There's always someone here. I'll mention it in roll call. Just tell the kids their Grandma's okay—we just need to get the tunnel cleared."

"But sir, that's not exactly true. She might not be okay." Makayla never lied.

"Officer Wainwright, that's how we're handling the situation. Do I make myself clear?" barked the Captain.

"Yes, sir, thank you, sir! Oh, and by the way, I like your tie!" Makayla beamed, glancing up at the Chief's standard-issue black tie.

"Get out of here!" Dupre roared, then winked and gave her a big grin.

∾

Simone sat at her desk, working on the next press briefing. She'd come to the conclusion there was really no way to prepare for these things. Nevertheless, she attempted to anticipate questions and formulate responses. Once again, a soft knock interrupted her thoughts. She looked up to see Earl Bentsen.

"Sorry to bother you, Ms. Perez. I just stopped by to let you know that a team of engineers has arrived and they're working with some fellas from my department down in the tunnels." Earl gave her a broad smile.

"Chief Bentsen, I am so glad you stopped by. Please, sit down, and have a cup of coffee."

"Gosh, I'd love a cup of joe. Can you spare the time?" Earl asked cautiously.

"Chief Bentsen, for you, I'll make time." Simone smiled.

"Call me, Earl," he said, wrestling off his fireman's slicker.

Simone returned in a moment with two piping hot cups of coffee. "And I'm Simone." He nodded and took a sip, and sighed with pleasure. Simone continued, "I wanted to thank you for helping me in the meeting. Vaughn Hanesworth is probably one of the best historic preservation architects in the country."

"One of the biggest pains in the butt, too!" Earl said. They both laughed. "I've worked with him for many years and I very rarely take him to task. However, we cannot allow intellectuals to get in the way of saving lives. Vaughn means well." He put down his cup. "So tell me, Simone, where're you from?"

"Well, I grew up in New York City. Actually, my mother died suddenly when I was two. The kind sisters of St. Bartholomew's Catholic Orphanage raised me."

"Wow that must have been tough. Do you have any siblings?"

"No, unfortunately, I don't, though I wish I did." Simone leaned over and placed her cup on the side table. "The sisters were very kind, though, and I actually received a top-notch education. I've always wished to be part of a big family. However, it was not to be."

"Boy, our upbringings are very different. I'm the fourth of thirteen kids, and I grew up in southeast D.C., not far from here. My father worked three jobs, so I rarely saw him. Everybody worked in my family. I started my first job selling papers on the street corner when I was seven years old. I made good money too, for a kid that age. However, my first love was always the firehouse. I suppose it's in my blood."

"How many children do you have?" Simone asked.

The Chief took a sip of coffee and chuckled. "Well, Leena and I have four kids of our own who are all grown and on their own, except for our youngest daughter who's at American University. We've fostered six other kids over the years. Leena's a social worker, and she's always looking out for kids who need some help. Moreover, the kids in the neighborhood have decided it's cool to hang out at Bentsen's. To tell you the truth, there's no telling who'll show up at our dinner table on any given night. I tease Leena that she takes in kids to strengthen our marriage. Because, if we're having an argument and kids show up, we stop bickering. By the time we're alone again, we've forgotten all about the disagreement."

"Gosh, that sounds very rewarding—and hectic! Leena sounds like a gem. Do you ever tire of having a full house?" Simone asked with a laugh.

"Sometimes. A few weeks ago I got up to go to work and there was the neighbor kid in my bathroom shaving. No explanation or anything! At breakfast, I laid down the law. It lasted three days!" Earl laughed and continued. "But Leena made me a Black Forest cake, so it worked out."

Simone chuckled and said, "Tell Leena I want the recipe!"

As if on cue, the Chief's radio went off, "Sir, we have a problem back here at the firehouse. Can you give me your 10–20?"

Earl shook his head and grinned, "I'd best go. I'll see you at our next meeting. Thanks for the coffee."

"The pleasure was mine, sir." Simone said.

❧

"Addie, honey, are you feeling okay?" Barbara asked.

"My shoulder's hurtin' me some. It must be gettin' on two o'clock. My boys come home at three-thirty. I sure wish I could call somebody. Do you think someone will stop by and help out? I mean, how they gonna know?"

"Don't worry, Addie. They'll be fine," Barbara said reassuringly. "Right now, I think you should eat something. It'll help keep your strength up."

"Nope. I'm just not hungry right now." She was quiet for a long while, her hands knotted in her lap. Then without warning she slumped over in her chair.

"Dan, quick! Give me that orange juice there in the fridge," Barbara barked. She shook Addie.

"Addie. Honey, please stay with me. Drink this now!"

"No—I'm not hungry," Addie mumbled.

"Addie Hutchison, you drink this right now!"

Barbara held the glass in front of her until Addie took it. Mumbling to herself, she swallowed the orange juice in a few gulps and wiped her hand across her mouth. Within a few minutes, she straightened up as if she'd been in a trance. "What happened?" she said, embarrassed. "Oh my, I lost it, didn't I?" She grimaced and shook her head.

"Addie, eat this sandwich right now. All of it. C'mon." Barbara was firm. "You're not going into diabetic shock on my watch!"

Dan looked on as Barbara coaxed her patient. As Addie's color began to return, so did her cheerful countenance.

"Well, looks like it's my turn to make a horse's patoot out of myself—huh, Mr. Bruce?" In spite of themselves, everyone laughed, and Bruce found himself laughing hardest of all.

"Is she going to be okay?" Bruce asked Barbara behind his hand.

"For now, Addie is fine. Still, she needs insulin. What just happened could have been much worse if we hadn't had the juice. We need to get that medicine, and soon."

Joel Carlson slumped in a pew of St. Matthew's Catholic Church on the Hill, peering at the stained-glass windows. Somehow, the images and colors were strangely soothing. He was not Catholic, but he needed to connect with something beyond himself. It had been more than an hour since the press briefing. As a reporter, he felt empathy for Simone Perez. This difficult situation required patience and time. However, Joel's emotions clouded his professional judgment. Barbara—the love of his life—was among the missing.

He slipped from the pew to the kneeler, and as he did, tears came to his eyes. "Oh God," he silently prayed, "You know me. Throughout my life, you've somehow been a guiding force. I'm not a church-goer, and you know there have been times in my life that I'm not proud of. Still, I've always believed that you're there, I really do. Now, I don't know if Barbara's okay or if I'll ever see her again. Please, let Barbara be all right. I don't ask this for myself—but she's so wonderful. No matter what happens between us, thank you for allowing me to find out what love, real love, is. Please be with all those on the recovery team. Thank you. Amen."

Joel wiped his eyes on the cuff of his sleeve and rose to leave. As he approached the door to leave the church, he noticed a small wooden box marked "Funds for the Poor." Quickly rummaging through his pockets, he found a twenty-dollar bill. He stuffed it into the box and swiftly exited the church.

❧

Jim Stenson jerked awake from a fitful sleep and pulled himself upright. He'd heard something. He sat still, listening intently, making certain it hadn't been a dream. Then he heard it again.

"Dan, Barbara, quick! Get me back over to the pipes."

"I don't hear a thing," Dan protested.

"Shhh, just listen," said Jim impatiently.

They held their breath. Then they heard the unmistakable crackle of walkie-talkies come through.

Dan quickly guided Jim over to the pipes and handed him the decrepit broom he'd used earlier that day. Jim loudly clanged "SOS," hoping to attract attention. Before he could begin the third SOS, a voice cried from some sort of amplified device, "Hello, SOS. Where exactly are you?"

Jim yelled, "This is the underground coffee shop. There are five people here, including Congresswoman Barbara Perkins."

"Is Addie Hutchison okay? This is Rob Tate with the Maintenance Department."

"Addie took a bad fall and has a broken shoulder. She's in dire need of insulin. How soon do you think it'll be before we're rescued?" Jim shouted.

"There's a team of folks working on this. It'll be a while, but I'll see what we can do about the insulin." Rob responded. He had no idea how they would ever deliver a package to the coffee shop.

Dom quickly added, "Please give us the names of all of the others in the coffee shop, as well as any loved ones you'd like us to contact. We'll be working throughout the night to free all of you. Rob and I are trying to figure out where all the survivors are located. There's a team of rescue workers digging through a massive amount of rubble. Rob's been able to work his way through a very narrow vent space which is above the tunnel. Let me ask you, are there other injuries?"

"Yes. Father Larson hit his head and Bruce Graham has a broken wrist. The Congresswoman and I are fine. Well, except for some frayed nerves!"

"Copy that!" Dom responded. "Listen, I have all of your contact information. Rob and I will be back again in about an hour. One more thing; I assume you have enough food and drink, right?"

"We have plenty of caffeine and carbs, so we won't starve. But this shop grows smaller every hour!" said Jim.

"Rob and I will be back. Hang in there. This is Dom Martinelli with the Maintenance Department, out for now."

"Rob, let's get you out of that space," Dom insisted. He somehow knew Rob badly needed a break.

6

PAUL DAVIS GUIDED THE car down the 295 corridor into the southeast neighborhood where Addie Hutchison lived. "So, what's the deal on these kids?" he asked.

"Well," Makayla answered, "Addie keeps them on a pretty short leash. Since they lost their parents in a car crash eighteen months ago, it's been pretty rough on all of them. I have to hand it to her, she gets these kids to church each and every Sunday. And they're nice boys."

"How old are they?" Paul asked. "I have four at home—so I know what to expect!"

"Tyrone is fifteen. He's a quiet kid, likes basketball. I don't think he's discovered girls just yet, although I'm sure he'd like to try. The twins, Jamal and James, are eight and have energy to burn. Sometimes, when I watch them I have to lay down the law, but once they understand the rules, they're usually willing to comply. The only thing that worries me about taking them to the office is they will get tired and bored." Makayla glanced over at Paul.

"Not a chance!" he laughed. "While you were busy talking to folks before roll call, your stellar partner got three old laptops and downloaded games. In addition, there's a pizza party at six o'clock, thanks to the Chief. Finally, I know how to deal with tired kiddos—there's never a dull moment at my house." Paul grinned. "One more question: How are these kids going to deal with me—a white cop—walking into the house?"

"There won't be an issue. If there is, I'll certainly set them straight!" Makayla laughed as Paul pulled up to Addie's house.

The neighborhood looked rough and run down. Old men were sitting on the corner, sharing a bottle they kept in a brown paper bag. Paul held the door for Makayla and walked up to Addie's front porch. Makayla knocked and then called out, "Tyrone, are you in there? It's me, Miss Makayla."

Before long, a tall, skinny kid opened the door a crack, but kept the safety latch on. "Hello, Miss Makayla. My Gran isn't home just yet. I'd ask you in, but she said not to let anybody in when she's not here."

Tyrone glanced at Paul, then quickly looked at Makayla.

"Listen to me, Tyrone," she said, "under most circumstances, I'd agree; you shouldn't let folks in when your grandmother's not here. However, you know me and we need to talk with you. So please open the door and let us in."

She stood back, her hand dropping to her side.

"Why do you need to talk to me? I've done nothing wrong."

The boy stood his ground.

Paul spoke quietly, looking Tyrone in the eye, "No one thinks you've done anything wrong at all, son. But there's been an accident at the Capitol and we need to help you make some decisions that will help your family." Paul's voice was kind, but firm. After a moment, Tyrone unfastened the chain and opened the door.

Paul and Makayla walked into the foyer. The living room looked neat as a pin, belying the fact that three boys lived there. Before she could say a word, James and Jamal bounded down the stairs squealing, "Miss Makayla's here!"

"Hi there!" Paul stooped down to their level, "I'm Officer Paul. I work with Miss Makayla. What grade are you fellas in?"

"We're in second grade!" Jamal answered, "And we like school, too. Cause we're very smart. Are you staying for supper?"

Paul chuckled, "Well, no, not this time. Let's go into your living room so that we can all talk, okay?"

Tyrone looked at Makayla, "Something's not right. Is Gran in the hospital or something?"

"No, honey. There's been an accident. Sit down and Officer Paul will explain."

Paul put James on one side and Jamal on the other, all the while maintaining eye contact with Tyrone. He took a deep breath and explained. "Boys, there has been a huge explosion at the Capitol. You've been to your Gran's shop and you know that it's in a tunnel."

Tyrone interrupted, "I bet some crazy guy tried to blow the Capitol up!"

Makayla explained, "Well, no. They have been installing a new electrical system. There was an explosion and the tunnel collapsed. A team of people is working very hard to clear the tunnel and rescue your Gran. Here's the thing; it's going to take some time and we don't know when your Gran will be home. We want the three of you to come with us back to our main office, and if your Gran isn't out at the end of my shift, you can spend the night at my house."

"Wow, Jamal. We get to stay at Miss Makayla's house and probably have pancakes for breakfast!" James seemed delighted with this arrangement.

Tyrone stood up and said, "I don't need a babysitter. You can take the twins, but I'm not going. Besides, I got . . . things to do."

"What things, boy?" Makayla demanded. "Are you working for the Man? Cause brother, if you are, I'm busting you thirty ways from Sunday!"

"No, Miss Makayla, I'm not working for some drug dealer. I'd never do that! This isn't about some girl, either. It's just . . ." Tyrone's voice trailed off. "Okay, look. Here's the truth. James and Jamal, you say one word about this to Gran, and you'll be walking funny for the next three months. They say to me, 'Tyrone, you're the man of the house now.' They don't know what Gran's up against. Money is tight, so sometimes Gran skips her medicine. So, I got a part-time job at CVS restocking shelves from ten p.m. till three in the morning. I knew if I asked Gran, she'd just say no. After everyone's down for the night, I slip out the back door. I've saved six hundred dollars so far. I wanted to save more and then give it to her."

Tyrone had tears in his eyes. Makayla knew he was telling the truth.

"Well, boy, aren't you a fine one!" Makayla walked over and put her arms around him. "Look, where's this CVS? How 'bout you and me go by your work and explain the situation. I really think—as the man of the house—your brothers need you to be with them."

"Well, that's true. I have homework, too," Tyrone volunteered.

Paul turned to the twins. "James and Jamal, show me where your clothes are. I bet you guys have some really cool *Star Wars* pajamas!"

He coaxed the twins upstairs to pack for the evening.

Rob sat in yet another meeting, lost in his own thoughts. He was exhausted and he missed his wife. Yet, he couldn't get Addie out of his mind. How in the world could he get a package of insulin into the coffee shop?

Dom had told the group about talking to those trapped inside the coffee shop. They discussed Barbara Perkins's confinement at length.

Somehow, having a member of Congress involved made the crisis worse. In the middle of Dom's presentation, Vaughn blustered in and took a seat.

Chief Bentsen had been in the middle of giving an update to the group about his work with the newly hired engineers working on the tunnel when, without thinking Rob shouted, "That's it! That will work."

When he realized what he'd done he smiled sheepishly and said, "Ms. Perez, Chief Bentsen, I'm so sorry for the outburst. However, I'm really worried we could lose Addie because of her diabetes. I think I've figured out a way to get a package down there. Like Dom said, this is an old building, with a lot of layers. I think there's a dumbwaiter running parallel to the water pipes. I'm pretty sure it dead-ends into the storage area in the coffee shop. I could get there that way."

Before anyone could respond, Vaughn spoke up. "I'm very sorry, but that idea is ill-advised and must be rejected out of hand. No one should touch something from antiquity. Certainly not a plebian maintenance worker!" He glared at Rob.

Simone jumped in before Rob could reply. "Excuse me, Vaughn, but this is a matter of life and death. Although I commend your efforts to preserve antiquity, I'm afraid I must overrule you on this."

"That's unfortunate," Vaughn shot back. "I'm sure you'll come to regret it."

Ignoring him, Simone continued, "Rob, you're certainly excused for the outburst. I have a couple of questions before we let you go." She smiled encouragingly at him. "Where do you think this dumbwaiter originates? And are you taking enough breaks?"

Rob said shyly. "If I am right, this dumbwaiter is in the Speaker's office. Can someone call and tell them I'm coming? I mean, this isn't some place I typically go."

Before Simone could answer, Dom volunteered, "I know that office very well from some repairs we recently did. I'll help Rob with this."

Simone nodded, "Are you folks taking enough breaks?"

Dom laughed. "Rob's the one doing all the work! All I'm doing is helping him broadcast the information so he can save his energy. While we have the floor, we have the contact information of those trapped in the coffee shop; who should I give that to? Assuming the dumbwaiter thing works out, who will pick up the insulin? If you give me the contact information, I can work with the infirmary to get the medicine."

"Nice work, young man!" Simone gave Rob a smile.

"Okay, everyone, it's four o'clock now and I'm holding a presser at five-thirty. I do not feel there is a need to reconvene our working group again today. However, I am asking that representatives from the Maintenance Department, D.C. Fire and Rescue, and Pickering Architects be present through the night. Please watch for a text from me making these arrangements final.

"Let's meet here tomorrow morning at eight a.m. sharp!"

Once the meeting had ended, Simone called her office as she walked out of the Capitol and told them she needed a quick break. She would be back in thirty minutes to prepare for the 5:30 press briefing. Usually, she enjoyed walking along the Mall, but not today. She had so much on her mind that she found it difficult to work through everything. She needed time to think and to sort out her feelings.

She found the cool October air refreshing as she walked briskly. Gradually, the knot in her stomach began to subside and soon she found herself at the Hirschhorn Sculpture Garden. She sat down and tried to compose herself. Something was troubling her—something that reached beyond the immediate crisis. If she'd had the time, she would have gone home to seek solace in her cello, playing something by Vivaldi to soothe her frayed nerves.

Am I really in over my head? Why am I so frightened?

Her professional instincts answered loud and clear. As an architect, she clearly understood the tasks at hand. She had complete confidence in her top-notch team. The press was another matter. Still, the Speaker had asked her to handle this, so handle it she would.

Simone glanced at her watch and got to her feet. As she walked back to the Capitol, she had a gnawing fear which she didn't fully understand. Then she asked herself a terrifying question: *What if they lose Addie? No*, she said to herself firmly, *that is not going to happen.*

She remembered when she first came to Washington to interview for this position she had stumbled upon the café. Addie had made her feel welcome immediately, and in no time the two women were chatting like old friends. They shared a love for cooking and regularly swapped recipes. Addie's friendship had offered Simone a refuge which she desperately needed. She shuddered as she realized that if she hadn't been running late, she too could be stuck in the café as a result of the explosion. She felt a pang of guilt, but she knew she had no time for such emotions.

She picked up her pace, and with it her resolve. *I will do everything in my power to save the victims of this explosion. Addie will be just fine!*

The ringing of her cellphone interrupted her thoughts.

"Simone, this is John. How's it going?"

For a moment, Simone did not recognize the Speaker's voice.

"John, I'm glad you called!" she exclaimed. She took a breath. "There's a press briefing at five-thirty. Can you join me there?"

"Maybe, if I'm not tied up with the DOD appropriations bill," he said hesitantly. "By the way, it's excellent news that they've found a way to get Addie's insulin to her."

"Yes, we're all really relieved. Will you say a few words to the press?" She wondered if it was presumptuous of her to ask.

"Of course, if I'm able to make it," he said. "Either way I'll see you this evening."

As she hung up, Simone realized John McIntyre didn't seem as aloof as she'd thought. She smiled to herself as she entered the Capitol and flashed her credentials to the Capitol cops on duty. Soon she was at her desk deftly preparing talking points for her remarks.

Rob followed Dom into the Office of the Speaker of the House. A woman sat at the receptionist desk and smiled at Dom as he walked in.

"Lillian Hawkins, how are you?" Dom boomed as they came through the door. "What a day this has been, huh? Lillian, meet Rob Tate. He's been dragging himself through a very narrow vent space trying to figure out where the survivors are."

"Mr. Martinelli! Good to see you again, although I wish it were under other circumstances. Hello Rob, it's nice to meet you. So, there are survivors?" Lillian pressed.

"Yep. There are five people trapped in that little coffee shop. You know the little café?"

"Gosh yes, I buy coffee from Miss Addie every day. How can we help?"

Dom nudged Rob.

"Well ma'am," Rob began, "there's an old space in this office that used to be a dumbwaiter. If my memory serves me right, it goes all the way down to the basement and into a supply closet in the coffee shop. Addie is a diabetic and she needs insulin bad, and if this works I think I can get some medicine down to her."

Lillian got to her feet. "Well, this is a bit unusual. The Speaker's in the middle of some important phone calls. Where exactly is this dumbwaiter located?"

"Um . . . it's in the Speaker's bathroom," said Rob.

Lillian nodded. "Do you know how long you'll need?"

Dom looked at Rob. "I'd say no more than ten minutes for now, ma'am," said Rob. "If this works, we'll need to come back and that might take longer."

"Wait here a moment." Lillian left and they heard her tap gently on the Speaker's door and say, "Mr. Speaker, Dom, the Director of Maintenance, and his assistant need access to your bathroom . . ." and that was all they heard as the door closed.

In a moment Lillian bustled back, "The Speaker says come right on in."

Rob walked through the plush office feeling awkward and tired. Before they could say anything, the Speaker stood up, smiling. "Gentlemen, please come right on in. You two bring the first good news of the day. Lillian tells me there are at least five survivors."

"Mr. Speaker!" Dom said, "It's nice to see you again. This is my associate, Rob Tate."

Rob held out his hand. "Hello, sir."

"Rob, you look very familiar. Have I ever met you before, young man?" the Speaker asked.

"No sir, not that I know of," Rob stammered.

"That's funny, because I never forget a face." He looked closely at Rob. "Members on both sides of the aisle tease me about that. Anyway, please, go right on into the bathroom."

Rob quickly found the space nestled under an ancient sink. He unscrewed the grid, grabbed his drop light and began lowering it slowly. It thrilled him when the light began to disappear. Then he heard a thud. The light had hit something solid.

"Dom, this may not work after all," he said anxiously. As he reeled the light back up, he saw there was a rope attached to two small pulleys on either side. He gently tugged on the ropes and to his surprise an actual dumbwaiter appeared.

"Yes!" Rob ducked back out from under the sink and quickly explained the situation to Dom. "Okay, Rob, you go back and explain to the folks in the coffee shop. Let's go!"

On their way out, Dom explained everything to Lillian and promised they'd return very soon. As they left the Speaker's office, Dom put his hand on Rob's shoulder. "How you holding up?"

Rob shrugged. "I'm okay, but I'm really frustrated. Everything takes so much time! And I haven't even gotten down to the mechanical room yet."

"Rob, listen to me; you're only one guy, right? You're doing a fabulous job. One thing at a time. Have you talked to Anna?"

"No, not yet," he sighed. "I need to get back up in the vent space and of course, there are all these stupid meetings taking up valuable time."

"Nope—I'm your boss; take forty-five minutes off. Get a Coke, call your wife, relax a bit. This is not all up to you, champ." Dom spoke to Rob more like a father than a boss. "You're the only one who's working in the vent space. I need you to keep up your strength. Take a short break and come to the meeting late. That's an order! I've got your back, buddy."

He clapped Rob on the back and hurried off to his office to put out other fires.

〜

Rob took a long drag on his cigarette and dialed Anna's number. "This is Anna Tate. May I help you?"

The minute Rob heard her voice, tears welled in his eyes.

"Hey babe," was the most he could muster.

"Oh, hi honey. How's your day going? Gosh, it's three forty-five. How come you're calling me? I'll see you at home soon."

Rob gulped. "You haven't heard any news today, have you? There was an explosion at the Capitol this morning." He heard her gasp and hurried on. "Don't worry, I'm fine. Most of the tunnel between the House and Senate collapsed. Since I'm so skinny, I'm the guy up in this tiny vent space trying to figure out if there are any survivors. I am not going to be able to come home tonight. I'm so sorry . . ." Rob's voice trailed off.

"Rob, when is your next break? I want to bring you dinner. Let me drop the girls off at my mom's.

"Anna, listen for a second. I want to see you too—more than you'll ever know. Still, I'm worried about the girls. I wonder if it'd be better if you stay home and just tell them I got the chance to do some overtime so we can go to Disney. Don't let them watch any TV, period, okay? The press is everywhere, and you know the girls would be really scared if they heard about this."

"Honey, what if I do this: I'll stay home and get Hanna and Laura to sleep. Then please let me come down for a few minutes about ten o'clock tonight." Anna's voice was warm.

"What if the kids wake up?" Rob asked.

"Maria will tell them I ran to Grandma's and I'll be back really soon," she said.

"Perfect! Bring some clean clothes, especially some shirts. You would not believe how dirty I am. I love you."

Rob hung up the phone and hurried to the meeting.

7

SIMONE STEPPED UP TO the podium and said, "Ladies and gentlemen, please take your seats." She waited a moment for the noise to subside and then continued. "First, I have some very good news. We have confirmed there are five people trapped in the small café that is located in the mid-section of the tunnel. They survived the explosion, and for the most part are doing fine. These five include Congresswoman Barbara Perkins, representative from Wyoming. Also trapped in the café are Addie Hutchison, the proprietor of the café, Father Dan Larson, Rector of St. Matthew's Episcopal Church in McLean, Bruce Graham, Counsel to the Senate Judiciary Committee, and Jim Stenson, who works for Blind Citizens United. The group is faring all right under the circumstances, but there are some injuries. It's my understanding that Ms. Hutchinson is a diabetic and is in dire need of insulin. The maintenance staff is exploring ways to get this medication to her as soon as possible. They believe an unused dumbwaiter will enable them to get medication to Addie."

Simone paused and looked down at her notes.

"On another matter, the Department of Homeland Security is lending us a device called FINDER, which stands for Finding Individuals for Disaster and Emergency Response. It works by emitting a low-powered microwave signal through the rubble. It can detect tiny motions caused by victims' breathing and heartbeats. This could be invaluable for helping us find victims. That piece of equipment should arrive on the Hill within the hour and will enable us to ascertain if anyone is trapped somewhere else within the tunnel.

"That is what we know at present. I will now take questions."

Amid the clamor, Simone recognized one of the reporters who jumped to his feet. "Ms. Perez, Joel Carlson with *The Washington Post*. Is the Congresswoman hurt in any way? As a follow-up, do we know how long it will take to free these folks?"

"To answer your first question, Joel," responded Simone, "the Congresswoman is not hurt. In fact, I understand she has a nursing degree and has been helping her fellow victims trapped in this unfortunate situation. As to your second question, that's very difficult to say. Captain Dupre, the head of the D.C. Fire and Rescue Department, Chief Bentsen, and/or their designees, will be here throughout the night. It's slow going because, on the one hand, they want to get to the survivors as soon as humanly possible. On the other hand, they must be careful that their rescue efforts do not injure the survivors."

Jane Spollen with the *New York Times* asked, "How did they initially make contact with the café? And on another topic, can you tell us if the Capitol is safe and when Congress will resume?"

Simone took a deep breath. "As you know by now, there's a vent space which dates back to 1864, if I'm not mistaken. One of our maintenance staff—Rob Tate—has inched himself through that vent space and made contact with the café survivors. We're using some technology developed by the Army that allows us to talk to survivors.

"Turning to the safety of the Capitol, we've called in the distinguished members of Pickering Architects. Some of you may recall this firm worked extensively on the recent renovations of the Capitol. They have spent most of the afternoon trying to ascertain if the Capitol sustained any structural damage. These architects need more time to be certain the building is safe. This, coupled with the need for the search-and-rescue team to do their jobs, has led the Speaker to announce the Capitol will remain closed until further notice."

Simone fielded several other questions and then added, "There are two other matters worth noting. First, thanks to the efforts of Congressman Chamberlin, families awaiting word about their loved ones are welcome to wait in Rayburn House office building 2330. We have worked with the Congressman's staff as well as the Chaplain of the Senate. Counselors will be there round the clock. Finally, please be aware that the House Pages—you know these wonderful young people who run errands which literally keep both chambers of the Congress going—are organizing an all-night vigil on the west front of the Capitol. It seems Ned Ramirez of New Mexico is among those persons missing. It would be really nice if some of you would cover this story since these are young people—most of whom are in their teens and far from home—and this is a difficult time for them.

"Thank you. We will give another briefing at eight p.m."

◆

When Rob climbed back into the vent space, nothing went as he had planned. For one thing, with all of his gear on it was almost impossible to breathe. Inching his way through the crawl space was even more difficult this trip. Once Rob was over the café and had established contact again, he explained that they had determined a way to get Addie the medicine she needed.

"This is what I need you to do, Jim," he called out. "There's a supply closet about fifteen feet to the left of these pipes. Inside that closet there's a fairly ornate register. It goes to an old dumbwaiter used in the original Capitol. You'll have to move some stuff around. Find a screwdriver, or something you can use as a screwdriver." He waited, holding his breath.

"I have a screwdriver in my briefcase," said Jim, "but I'll need to get Dan to help me find the register."

"Why's that?" Rob asked.

"Oh, right, I forgot to tell you: I'm blind. However, I can do this. No problem."

Rob wondered silently what else could complicate things further. Still, Jim seemed to understand what he needed to do.

Rob tried to move further down the vent space, hoping to reach the mechanical room. Again, his efforts failed. He became stuck and twice he had to ask Dom to pull him out. Tired and discouraged, Rob climbed out of the vent space and announced, "Dom, I need to go make a personal call. I'll meet you upstairs in ten minutes. I'll be a little late for the meeting."

With that, Rob went to his truck and called his AA sponsor, Evan. When he answered, Rob quickly explained the day's events, closed his eyes and said, "Evan, buddy, the pressure I'm under tonight is unbelievable. All I can tell you for sure is this: I really want a drink. Please help me."

They talked for a while until Rob began to breathe easier. Then Evan prayed, not for the crisis, but for Rob, saying, "God, my brother Rob's trying to do all this by himself. God, only you can get Rob through this night and you're far more powerful than any drink Rob might think he needs. Please help him, Lord, to let go and let You work through him." Then he said, "There's an AA meeting in Room 301 in the Cannon House Office

Building. It meets at seven tonight. You get yourself to that meeting and I'll call you later!"

And with that, Evan hung up.

❧

For the first time since the explosion, the café sat quiet. Addie lay napping on a makeshift pallet Father Dan and Barbara had put together for her. Jim Stenson sat engrossed in a talking book he'd downloaded to his phone months ago. Bruce sat studying a legal opinion.

After checking on Addie, Barbara sat down at a table with Father Dan. "So, how's your headache? Caffeine sometimes helps. May I get you some coffee, Father Dan?"

"No, thanks Barbara. I've had quite enough coffee for one day. My head still hurts, but it's not as bad as before. Looks like neither of us are going to make it home for dinner, huh?"

"Not looking like we'll even get out of here before tomorrow. At least we have food. Tell me about your family, Dan. Do you and your wife have children?"

"Colleen and I have a daughter, Amy, who's the joy of my life! She'll be graduating from George Mason University in May. She's a really good, responsible kid. I'm not just saying that—she's almost more responsible than her parents. For example, this morning, as I'm leaving for this Hill meeting, Amy made me promise we'd talk tonight about graduate school. I mean, this kid has almost a year to figure this out. That's my girl. How about you, Barbara? Do you have kids?" Dan asked.

"No, unfortunately. Paul and I weren't able to have children," Barbara said, "but as it all turned out, I'm thankful no one else had to endure losing him."

"So, if you don't mind my asking," said Father Dan, "How are things going for you now? Your husband has been gone for a while, right?"

"Five years," Barbara said, looking at him. "At first I found it hard—really hard. Assuming Paul's Congressional seat challenged me. It gets easier as you go along. Lately . . . well, it hasn't been as lonely either."

"Oh, and why's that, Congresswoman Perkins?" Dan asked with a mischievous grin.

"Well, you're a priest, so you keep secrets, right?" Barbara asked earnestly.

"Gosh yes. As a priest, folks are free to tell me anything, though there are times when I wish some of my parishioners would keep some things to themselves," he said with a smile.

"Well . . ." Barbara began hesitantly. She glanced around to make sure no one could hear. "I've been seeing a guy who actually is a reporter for *The Washington Post*. We met at one of those seminars the Library of Congress puts on and one thing led to another. He's so different from Paul. I mean whereas Paul was a go-getter, Joel is more thoughtful and deliberate. He loves the outdoors! Joel makes me very happy." She paused. "There's just one problem."

"What's that?" Dan asked.

"Joel is very serious about our relationship. On several occasions he's hinted we should get married. I love him—I truly do. However, Paul will always be the love of my life. I gave my heart to him twenty-two years ago. Although I love Joel, I somehow don't see myself making that commitment again." She looked down at her hands. Changing the subject, she said, "Tell me about your wife."

"Well, we've been married for twenty-eight years—and still on the honeymoon!" Dan laughed. Then his smile faded. "I hope she knows I'm okay. This'll be hard on her—that's for sure."

"So, how did you two meet? Let me guess—college I'll bet!" Barbara smiled.

"Actually, I agreed to work at an Episcopal camp the summer after I got a bachelor's degree in Business Administration. Colleen was the Assistant Director. We fell in love, and by the end of the summer I'd asked her to be my wife. In fact, I spent almost my entire earnings that summer on her diamond ring. My dad teased me that that ring became the best investment of my life. He got that right. She really is the love of my life!" Dan smiled.

"So, how did you end up as a pastor?" Barbara asked.

"Well," Dan continued, "that same summer Father Jack Reynolds served as the Director of that camp. He was a pastor for thirty years and he also loved the outdoors. Every time he preached, he left me wanting more. That's when I realized how deep my faith had become. Jack and I became fast friends, so I wasn't too surprised when he sent for me one afternoon. I was surprised to meet his bishop, who handed me an application to his seminary. It stunned me when he said, 'Dan, you have a gift for putting people at ease. You're smart and you're committed, and I want you to seriously think about going to seminary.' So, after camp was over, I focused on marrying Colleen and becoming a holy guy!"

"Wow!" Barbara exclaimed. "You began your married life at seminary? Talk about making radical changes to one's life!"

"Well," said Dan, "both of us went through a period of adjustment. Looking back on it, I think those three years were some of the best years of our marriage."

Barbara straightened and said, "Father Dan, you're a good man and I think your parishioners are very lucky to have you. In fact, one day you just may look out into your congregation and see Joel and me sitting in a pew!"

"That would be a real honor, Barbara. Perhaps the four of us could go out afterwards for supper somewhere. For me, there's nothing like a good meal after I preach."

❧

James and Jamal sat side by side in the same office chair playing a game of Where's Waldo on the computer. Officer Paul sat nearby at his desk answering the seemingly endless stream of phone calls. Tyrone tried to concentrate on the paper he was writing for his civics class. The office teemed with activity since many of the officers from the day crew had agreed to work a double shift. Tonight, the Capitol Police had to assist in the search-and-recovery efforts, escort family members, and above all, keep the Capitol safe. All of this transpired as the officers watched over Addie Hutchinson's grandkids.

"I wonder what's taking so long!" Jamal exclaimed. "If I had a bull-dozer, I'd plow right through there. People are gonna get hungry soon. You know how Gran gets when she has to wait for dinner. It's not pretty."

"Yeah, but they probably have a lot to think about. Anyway, I'm just glad we're staying at Miss Makayla's tonight," said James, "Hey! I just found Waldo and that means I won. He's right there! Got you, Jamal!"

"That's not fair! You cheated!" cried James.

"You two little bros quiet down!" Tyrone immediately stood up. The boys knew he meant business. "James, Jamal, these folks have gone out of their way to help us. These are busy cops. You two turn the volume down and let them work. In fact, turn that computer off now, you hear me? James, you got a reading book in your backpack, right? Jamal, I want you to work on your multiplication tables. Just turn off that game and get to your homework."

"But we're not going to school tomorrow," Jamal protested. "Least, I don't think so."

"Do your homework or they won't let you eat," said Tyrone, winking at Officer Paul.

As the two younger boys settled down to their homework, Paul walked over and sat on the edge of Tyrone's desk.

"Man, you rule with an iron fist, big brother!"

"Somebody has to lay down the law," Tyrone laughed. It pleased Paul to see the boy finally relax.

"So, what's your paper on, Tyrone?" Officer Paul asked.

"Well, it's about the First Amendment and the freedom of the press. All they do these days is get folks all riled up. So, I'm having a tough time defending these bozos."

"Well, Paul reflected, "have you ever talked to a newspaper reporter?"

Tyrone shook his head.

"Would you like to? I have a good friend who's a reporter here on the Hill. He and I belong to a motorcycle club. If you want, I can call and see if he's still here. Maybe he could give you some help on your paper. What do you think?" Paul asked.

"Will he tell me about the motorcycle, too?" Tyrone asked with a grin.

"I'm betting he would! Hang on," Paul took out his cellphone.

"Carlson," Joel answered.

"Well, well," said Paul "I see *The Washington Post's* finally getting its money's worth out of you. I'm glad you're still here."

"Hey, Paul." Joel smiled, "I'm staying all night. How can I help you?"

"All night? Can they make you do that?" Paul asked.

"Well, no. Let's just say I have my reasons. What's up?"

"Look, I need a favor. I have a young fellow here who's writing a paper on the First Amendment. Could you stop by and chat with him? He's Addie's grandson."

"Wow, sure," said Joel. "Addie's one of the few women who knows how I like my coffee. Sure, I'll be down soon."

"Well you'd best get a move on, brother. Pizza delivery guy just left." Paul laughed.

"On my way," said Joel. "Save me a slice of pepperoni!"

❧

Lillian Hawkins settled the three staffers from the Congressional Budget Office into a large conference room adjacent to the Speaker's office. She explained the Speaker would be there shortly, and offered them coffee and soft drinks. The CBO fellows were happily crunching numbers—their life's work.

Finally, the Speaker hurried in, looking more than a bit frazzled. "Mr. Speaker," Lillian caught him before he sat down. "Give me just two minutes before your CBO meeting."

"Sure, Lillian. What can I do for you? I suppose the better question is what have you done for me?" The Speaker managed a weary smile.

"Mr. Speaker, I called Julie, as you requested. She was glad that I called, but she's still concerned about you, as any daughter would be."

John tried to interrupt, but Lillian held up her hand.

"Let me finish. I told her you'd call her this evening. You should probably call all of your kids tonight, just to set their minds at ease. You have twenty-odd phone calls to return—only two of which are really important. Secretary Anderson at HHS needs an emergency authorization to order more flu vaccine. Apparently, this year's flu season is going to be much worse than previously expected. His staff will fax us the language first thing in the morning. Congressman Riley has some urgent national security matters he wants to discuss with you. I told him to expect a call around nine tonight," she said, as the Speaker grimaced. "Finally, I took the liberty of having your housekeeper bring some fresh clothes for you as well as some blankets. All of these things are in your personal closet. I left a menu of take-out options on your desk. If you decide now what you'd like, I can order food for you before I leave.

"Now, how else may I help you?" Lillian gave him a smile.

"Mrs. Hawkins," said John earnestly, "whatever I pay you, it isn't nearly enough! You always know what I'll need. Shouldn't we get married or something?"

Lillian blushed and said, "Mr. Speaker, we'd kill each other within a week. Besides, Vern needs me to fix his dinner, not to mention keeping our three kids straight! I'm planning to leave after your meeting starts. What else will you need this evening, sir?"

"Nothing, I guess," the Speaker said. "I have these fellas from CBO to deal with, then there's a final press briefing at eight o'clock I'd like to attend. For food, just get me a burger and fries. Today's a great excuse to splurge."

Lillian looked at him intently. "Mr. Speaker, it is Monday night."

John looked up, momentarily befuddled, then said, "Oh, right! I have AA at seven. It's going to be tight, but I can go and still make the press conference. Thanks Lillian."

He grinned up at her, sheepishly. Growing up as a preacher's kid, his father never allowed liquor or any kind of alcohol. During law school, John began to drink, and he took to it voraciously. His wife was five months pregnant when she explained he had two options. Either go to AA or she would leave. He made the decision without a regret. All of Washington knew this about the Speaker and most respected him for his stark honesty.

"Lillian, thanks for everything. Give Vern my best. I'll call Julie this evening. Let me go deal with the wonks from CBO."

"Get some rest, Mr. Speaker. I'll be here by eight tomorrow. Call me if you need me. I'll have dinner delivered at eight-thirty. Good night, Mr. Speaker."

8

WHEN ROB TATE REENTERED the vent space at about 6:15 p.m., everything seemed different somehow. He crawled through with ease, and it seemed like no time at all before he reached the café. "Hello Jim," he called. "How's life in the coffee shop this evening?"

Jim chuckled. "Actually, we're fighting over who gets the last roast beef sandwich! Look, we got the supply closet emptied and removed the old register. We're ready for the insulin. How's this going to work?"

"Okay, Jim," Rob said. "For this part of the operation, we're going to have a three-way call. My boss, Dom, is also on the line."

"Hey Dom. I gotta tell you, this guy Rob's the best. I think I speak for us all when I say Rob is wonderful. Give the man a raise!" Jim joked.

"I'm working on it," replied Dom without hesitation. "Jim, we've checked and the space is clear. Rob's lowering the package of insulin now. I say package because we've worked with Addie's doctor and it has the proper dosage plus the needle and syringe. Can you just stick out your hand? We should be able to literally put it in the palm of your hand."

Jim thrust his hand through the opening, but for a long time he felt nothing. Then he felt the package—no bigger than four by eight inches and shrink wrapped tightly—drop gently into his hand.

"Houston, the package is safely in my hand and its contents will be administered to Addie Hutchison in five minutes or less." Jim said.

"Nice job, everybody!" Dom exclaimed. "Please tell Addie, the Speaker sends his wishes for her very speedy recovery. Oh, and one more thing: Addie gets the roast beef sandwich, you knuckleheads!"

With that, the three-way call erupted into much-needed laughter.

$\sim$

Rob slipped quietly into Cannon Room 301 and took a seat in the next-to-last row. There were only six people: two women chatting together and four men wearing dress shirts, open at the collar, having long since discarded their neckties. Rob felt self-conscious and out of place in his work shirt clearly identifying him as "Capitol Maintenance Staff."

He looked up when a tall man with greying hair walked in and took his place. One of the women stood up and said, "Good evening and welcome to the Capitol Hill AA meeting. My name is Cindy and I'm an alcoholic. It's been eight years since my last drink." Everyone applauded. Then, one by one, each person stood up and gave their first name and the length of their sobriety. When the grey-haired man stood up to give his name, Rob recognized the Speaker of the House. Immediately, he thought of bolting—but the Speaker had already seen him so, when it came his turn, Rob stood and said, "Hey everyone. I'm Rob and I'm an alcoholic. I'm sober for ten years."

Cindy said, "Aren't you the fellow everyone's talking about? I think you're working in some vent space trying to find survivors of today's explosion."

"Yes ma'am," Rob said, rather embarrassed.

"Well thanks, because that's really got to be a hard job," Cindy said, smiling. "Thanks for all you're doing." She turned to the group, "Okay, tonight's meeting centers around Step Three. We turned our will and our lives over to the care of God as we understood Him. This is often one of the most difficult steps an AA member must take. I mean, all of us in this room at one time or another struggled with this because the hallmark of any good drunk is the notion that, 'Hey, I got this,' am I right?" Everyone chuckled and nodded. Cindy was clearly a talented leader who Rob couldn't help but like.

As they went around the room each member reflected on the third step. Some gave lengthy testimonials, others barely spoke at all. When the Speaker's turn came, he mused, "You know, it's very timely that we're on the third step this evening, given the events of today. When I joined AA thirty-five years ago, I didn't have a problem with this step. I'm the son of a Methodist preacher and that's my upbringing. Today, it's really been difficult for me; all those folks who may be trapped in the tunnel. All those staff trying to save the victims. Cindy is once again reminding me to let go and let God. So thank you Cindy—I needed to hear this."

When it came Rob's turn to speak, he stood and said, "Well, I didn't plan to be at this meeting tonight. I am working on the rescue effort. It's very slow going and I'm frustrated with myself, with the process, with everything. So frustrated in fact that—to be really honest, I wanted a drink. I wanted it bad. So I called my sponsor and, well, here I am. So thank you all for helping me see it's not up to me. I'm really just there to help Him." Rob sat down.

Rob turned to leave once the meeting concluded. Then he heard the Speaker of the House say, "Hey, Rob, wait up. Let's walk together."

"Sure," said Rob, turning to wait for the Speaker.

"So, you headed home now?" the Speaker asked.

"No, sir. I'm planning to work all night. I mean, just like you said at the meeting, we've got to find and rescue the victims," Rob replied.

"Well, look," John said, "I'm sticking around too. If you need anything, just come by. I understand Addie received her medication. Thank you for that."

As they walked toward the Capitol, the Speaker stopped and put his hand on Rob's shoulder. The dome of the Rotunda stood out against the night sky. "Look at that," he murmured. "Even on the toughest days that building's just a sight to behold."

"Yes, sir, it is. It surely is," Rob replied.

The Speaker asked, "So, Rob, you have any kids?"

"I have the three most beautiful girls in this world," Rob smiled. He was beginning to feel more at ease around the Speaker. They walked on, talking and laughing.

Dom entered the basement of the Rayburn Building where Simone Perez and her staff had set up a temporary office. He stuck his head in the door and saw Simone was in the middle of what seemed to be an important conversation. Still, she motioned him to sit as she said, "I understand your concerns, Congressman Fletcher, but it is not possible for me to project when we will be able to open the Capitol. I will certainly let you know . . ."

He could not hear the other side of the conversation. Simone raised her voice and said, "Listen to me, Congressman! At this moment, I am not concerned about your hearing. At this very moment, people are gathering to receive word about their loved ones. You know what, some of those people may not receive good news. If you'll excuse me, I have more pressing matters to attend to. I will gladly call you back when this crisis is over."

Simone hung up the phone and buried her head in her hands.

After a moment, she glanced up wearily. "Dom, please tell me you have good news! I've been fielding the most bizarre questions including– get this—how will this explosion affect the bird life around the Capitol grounds. How should I know?" Her voice rose an octave.

Dom chuckled, "Better you than me! I thought my office got all the wacko calls." He straightened up and smiled then. "I do come with good news! We were able to get the insulin down to Addie. I'd assume she's already received the medication. I just thought I'd let you know." Dom stood up to leave.

"Please, Dom, wait. Let's chat a bit." Simone motioned. "I've got a few questions."

Reluctantly Dom sat, looked at Simone, and said, "You know, I've worked on the Hill for thirty-six years and I've seen my share of bad days. But this one takes the cake—hands down."

"Your staff hasn't flinched—not once," Simone offered. "They're all just stepping up to the task. I don't mind telling you Rob Tate is one of your best. He thinks outside of the box, that's for sure. It would have taken you or me a week to think about using the dumbwaiter—no offense."

"None taken. Rob's one of my hardest workers. He's always had a sixth sense about what will work. That's why I hired him. Listen, I have a suggestion for tonight. May I speak freely?" Dom said.

"By all means." Simone replied.

"I think you should go home and get some sleep tonight," Dom said earnestly. He continued, "Look, this crisis isn't going to be over tonight. Chief Bentsen will be here and he's one of the best. He and I can handle things. If I need you, I have your cellphone. Believe me, this is the way to go."

Simone looked doubtful.

"Besides," he continued, "Only a handful of engineers are working through the night. I'm not planning to leave until after this fiasco is over!" Dom gave a weary smile.

Simone nodded then. "I'm holding a press conference at eight p.m.," she said, "and I'm staying for the vigil that the House Pages are holding. I think I'll let my staff go home so they can come in early. I'll just sleep here at my desk," Simone said.

"You're carrying a lot," Dom persisted. "You're updating the press every four hours, working with the Speaker, dealing with the interagency folks and so on. Why don't you make me the 'designated official' from ten p.m. to eight a.m.? Go home after the press conference and get some sleep. Tomorrow's not going to be much easier."

"What about you?"

"Listen," Dom explained. "We have some nice old couches in my office and I can sleep anywhere. Besides, right after I retire in six weeks, my youngest daughter Tina's getting married. My wife's sewing all of the dresses—including the wedding dress. Our house is full of giddy young bridesmaids and weary young boyfriends wondering what they're in for. Trust me, they won't even notice Pop's not home."

Simone smiled, "Man, I must tell you the idea of going home to a hot bath and a very tall drink sounds great! But let's stay in touch throughout the night, okay?"

"Absolutely. Give me your cell and we can trade texts throughout the night. If something big happens, I will definitely call," Dom promised.

"Bless you, Dom," said Simone gratefully.

∽

Joel Carlson took a bite of pepperoni pizza and chased it with a long swig of Coke. This day had been an eternity already, and although he knew Barbara was alive and reasonably well, he could not go home. Not until Barbara was safe and sound.

"So, John, these three boys are Addie's grandkids?" he asked, taking another bite.

"Yep," Paul replied. "They're good kids. The two little guys are getting tired and fidgety. They're only eight, and more than likely Addie usually has them almost ready for bed by now. Makayla will be taking 'em for tonight—but she's busy managing the garage where families of the victims are coming in. So, why are you staying late?"

"Well," said Joel, with a sheepish grin as he looked around him, "A woman—actually a woman who's very special to me, is one of the victims. She's okay, but I have no intention of leaving here until she's free."

"Well, my goodness!" laughed Paul. "You mean the great Joel Carlson, writer for *The Washington Post* and scholar of the House, has finally fallen for a woman! Man, I knew you were up to something because you haven't been bugging me about motorcycles for a while now."

Just then John's phone rang and in the distance Joel could hear the Chief yell, "Could someone please give these two boys something to do?"

"Tell you what." Joel said. "Let me take these three kids for a walk. There's a park three blocks away. The little fellas can run until they're tired, and I'll talk to the older boy about the joys and sorrows of the press. Just make sure Makayla has my cell number."

Paul looked at him with relief. "Hey James, Jamal, and Tyrone, come here please. This is my buddy, Mister Joel. He's a writer and a good guy. He knows where there's a playground! So why don't you guys go get some fresh air. You do whatever Mister Joel or Tyrone say, okay?" Paul admonished.

"Yes, sir. Are you really a writer?" James asked, turning to Joel. "Cause maybe you can write a book report for me!"

Before Joel could answer, Tyrone said, "Boy, I know you didn't just ask this gentleman to do your homework!" Then, turning to Joel, he said, "I'm sorry, sir."

"Doesn't bother me," Joel said, walking his three young charges toward the door. "So, I understand you have an interest in the First Amendment," Joel commented to Tyrone, as he guided the younger boys to the park.

Simone walked into the Speaker's Office to inform him about the arrangements she and Dom had worked out for the evening. Through his office door Simone could hear him on the phone discussing the future of the Department of Defense appropriations bill. She heard him say, "I completely understand, Ezra. Right now, my priority is to get everyone out of the collapsed tunnel, and make certain there are no casualties. This bill—as important as it is—will have to wait until this crisis is over. . . . I understand. . . . Sure, I'll give you a call and give you a head's up when we can get back to working on the bill. . . . Look, I must go. There's someone waiting to talk to me. . . . Yes, thanks.

"Hello, Simone, please come right on in," John said brightly, jumping to his feet. "Tell me, what's the latest?"

Simone gave a weary smile and said, "Mr. Speaker, I mean John, there's not too much that's newsworthy. I will tell you Dom is impressed with the work Chief Bentsen and the engineers have done in assessing the tunnel damage. Dom suggested—insisted really—I leave him in charge this evening so I could go home for a while. Are you comfortable with this arrangement, sir? I can stay on the premises if you prefer."

John gave her a broad smile. "I'm glad Dom's helping us make smart decisions! I totally agree with him. You need some rest; go home. But please, do me a favor and stop calling me, sir! It makes me feel old!"

Simone couldn't help but laugh. "I'm sorry, John. The Catholic nuns who raised me insisted on proper speech at all times."

"Well," he chuckled, "I'm Methodist, so I won't be reporting you to the nuns anytime soon. Go home, sleep. Tomorrow is likely to be just as challenging as today."

"That's exactly what Dom thinks," Simone replied. Then she asked, "When will you go home, John?"

"Well," he said. "I'm not going home until this is resolved. As Speaker, I feel I should stick around. I'm a widower, so no one is waiting for me. Besides, I have plenty of work to do on the Defense Appropriations bill.

Simone nodded, then said tentatively, "John, how long ago did you lose your wife? I hope I'm not being too forward."

"No, no, you're fine," he reassured her. "I became Speaker of the House twenty-two years ago. I'd leave home at five a.m., work hard all day, make the requisite cocktail rounds and get home well after eleven, only to do it all again the following day. I kept that pace up for over a year. Then I got a call from my wife, Diane. They'd admitted her to the hospital for 'routine tests.' Those routine tests revealed pancreatic cancer. Three months later, she was gone."

Simone winced and then leaned forward, "I'm so sorry, John. That's a very personal story. How old were your children when your wife got sick? I'm just trying to imagine you as Speaker, with three children who must have needed you very much."

John nodded. "My eldest daughter, Julie, was a sophomore in college. My son, Timothy, was in tenth grade and at the really awkward age boys go through when they're not really men, but neither was he a little boy either. Our baby, Ellie, had just entered seventh grade. I seriously considered resigning as Speaker. The guy I was talking to before you came to my office, Ezra Martin, got me through. Ezra told me not to worry—he had my back. Simone, Ezra basically ran the House while I helped the kids work through their mother's death. It was the kindness and prayers of thousands of people—especially Ezra—that carried us.

"Also, Herb Leventhal became an extraordinary friend," John added,

"Seriously? I mean isn't he a really conservative guy. How did he help?" Now Simone was curious.

"When Herb learned about Diane, he made an appointment to see me. I go into this meeting thinking he's going to tell me how I and the Democratic Party were all wet, et cetera. We went into my office, and sat down and he said: 'John, I have reserved this time on your calendar every week for the next six months. I know how difficult it is to lose a wife to this disease. I lost my Esther to breast cancer three years ago. I'm coming just to talk as a friend. We'll check our respective party affiliations at the door. Sometimes you'll want to talk, sometimes you won't. There will be times that you'll cry—and that's okay. Your kids are going to put you through the wringer. I'll be here. Nobody but the two of us will know about these meetings.'" John spread his arms wide. "So, Ezra Martin—a guy from inner city St. Louis and Herb Leventhal a guy from L.A.—both helped me get through the toughest time of my life."

Simone glanced at her watch and stood to her feet. She smiled shyly, "That's really something. I never would have guessed."

"Listen," she said quietly, "I need to go."

"Of course, Simone," said John. "Now, if you could, please tell our friends in the press I send my regrets, but that I do appreciate all they are doing to accurately and fairly report this situation."

"Certainly, John, I'll be pleased to do that. I'll probably head home right after the eight o'clock press briefing. I plan to be at work no later than eight tomorrow morning. The first press conference will be at ten. Please call if you need me," Simone said, over her shoulder.

"Good night, Simone. Rest well," John replied. As she left his office, he couldn't help but notice her tall slender body silhouetted against the evening light.

9

ADDIE TOOK A BITE of her roast beef sandwich and ate it slowly, savoring the experience. "I'm sure grateful to God—and all of you—for gettin' me that insulin. I still can't believe how they got it down here." She took another bite.

"Rob explained everything to me step by step." Jim said. "Dan and I moved stuff in your supply closet. We'll fix the mess tomorrow."

"Now, did all of you get something to eat? There's more sandwiches in the back fridge. They always send extras," Addie said.

"Hallelujah!" exclaimed Dan. He went to the back and returned with an armload of subs and sandwiches. "Okay, boys and girls. We have two—no three—roast beef sandwiches, a couple of Italian subs, and three egg salads, fresh this morning. At any rate, they're certainly safe to eat."

Bruce cleared his throat. "May I please have one of the subs? I mean if no one else minds."

"Sure, Mr. Bruce." Addie said. "How you feeling? You made some progress on that memo?"

"Well, some, Addie," Bruce replied. "It just that . . . well I can't write so well with my swollen wrist. Man, I've learned one thing: always keep a couple of cheap paperbacks in my briefcase. I have some legal journals I can read," Bruce said.

"So, Jim, I've been wanting to ask you something since this morning," Dan began tentatively.

"Go ahead," said Jim Stenson. "Ask away."

"Well," said Dan, "how exactly does a blind guy jog ten miles, with traffic and all?"

Jim smiled and shot back, "Very carefully."

After they erupted in laughter, Jim continued. "This morning, I jogged with my next-door neighbor. He needs to drop forty-five pounds, so he hired me as his trainer. I make him jog ten miles a day and he makes sure

I stay alive. Seriously, that's one of the reasons we live in Rosslyn. You see, that city has audible pedestrian signals which sends out a signal I can hear when the light's red. So my wife—who's also blind—and I can easily navigate the streets. I work for Blind Americans United as the Director of Legislative Affairs."

Jim Stenson's professional qualifications were impeccable. He held a Master's in Political Science from Loyola and had spent many years in the trenches working as a research assistance for Congresswoman Anne Daniels. Then he landed an interim position as Assistant Director of Legislative Affairs for a human service coalition. Two years ago, Blind Americans United had asked him to become its director of legislative affairs.

"I've heard good things about your agency," Barbara said. "From what I've read—and I read far more widely than my staff gives me credit—you guys really do outstanding work."

"Well, Congresswoman," replied Jim, "I'm really pleased you think highly of us. Perhaps I can meet with your staff—I mean when we get out."

"Forget talking to my staff, Jim!" Barbara said with a smile. "If you need something—anything—come directly to me. I'll give you my cell number. The one thing I hate about being a Congresswoman is staff! I mean they're wonderful and they all work hard, but God bless 'em, they don't talk to me. I mean, last night's a prime example. The DOD appropriations bill was supposed to be on the House floor today. I had a big-time amendment. So what do my staff do? They gave me a six-inch thick briefing book that I sat up half the night reading. I wish they'd just talk to me!"

"Well," Jim responded. "Have you ever told them how you'd like to receive your information? My hunch is—and I hope you don't mind my saying this—but I'll bet that's how your late husband preferred to receive his information."

Barbara paused, and then said, "Jim, you are absolutely right! I'm not sure why that never occurred to me before. What can I do now? I mean they're used to cranking out these books. Who am I to tell them to stop?"

"You're the Congresswoman, that's who!" said Jim emphatically. "Your staff work for you, not the other way around. If they give you information that doesn't meet your needs, then I'd say you're not fulfilling your obligation to your constituents. I'd stop the production of these books and ask for two-page memos, coupled with face-to-face meetings with staff. Tell them it's okay to talk to you. I'd even set aside a couple of hours a week when your staff can come in and just chat. Then, if there's a need for any sort of briefing material, they can give you briefing folders. You know, stuff that can be read in one sitting."

"Gosh," exclaimed Barbara, "I ought to hire you as my communications director. I'm only half kidding."

"Well, I'm really not looking for a job, but we can chat," Jim replied. "For now, I'm wondering just how long we'll be trapped here. When I put that question to Dom, he said they'd have a rescue team working all night. So, it'll be sometime tomorrow before they reach us."

"Addie," Jim called out, "do we have enough food to last for a day?"

Addie thought for a moment. "Yes, we should have plenty. But we should watch and not eat too much right now."

"You're right, Addie," said Barbara. "Still, you need to eat several small meals so you keep your strength up."

"Yes ma'am. You know what?" Addie turned to look toward the back of the cafe. "We have some emergency provisions. I think there may be some blankets back there somewhere. Let me go and look."

She stood stiffly, but a new wave of pain made her drop heavily back down in her seat.

"Addie, don't worry!" Dan said, jumping to his feet. "Jim and I will go find them. We're getting pretty good at this."

❧

Joel Carlson and Tyrone Hutchison walked toward the briefing room. Before they entered, Joel said quietly, "Listen, when we go in there, they'll probably ask you your name. Just say Tyrone. If they find out you're Addie's grandson, they'll ask you a million questions. I don't think you're interested in recounting your family's history right now"

"No, sir. Thanks, Mr. Joel."

They slipped quietly into the briefing room and took their seats in the third row. Numerous reporters were milling around, obviously exhausted from a tiring day.

"Hey Joel, are you going to this vigil the pages are holding?" asked Dave Dickerson of *USA Today*.

"I thought I would," said Joel. "By the way, Dave, this is my friend Tyrone. He's doing some research for a school paper on the First Amendment. I thought I'd bring him here to see you clowns in action."

"Ah, the First Amendment is highly overrated," Dave said, extending his hand. "Nice to meet you, young man. So, where do you go to school?" Dave asked.

"I, ah, I go to Roosevelt, sir," said Tyrone.

"How's your football team? I mean, isn't that what's important at any high school?" Dave asked with a grin.

"To tell the truth, our football team isn't that great, but we're unbeaten in basketball," Tyrone replied. He looked up with a smile.

Dave opened his mouth to ask another question just as an attractive, well-dressed woman walked up to the podium. He quickly took a seat.

"Good evening, ladies and gentlemen," said Simone Perez. "In case there's someone here who missed our previous briefings, I'm Simone Perez, Architect of the Capitol. This press briefing will be mercifully short."

She paused and smiled as an appreciative murmur arose.

"It's been a very long day and there's actually not much new to report. Before I begin, I must tell you the Speaker asked me to send his greetings to you. As you know, the D.C. Fire and Rescue Department, the Capitol Maintenance Department, and some newly hired engineers are working in tandem to clear the tunnel and assess its structural integrity. A team of workers will be working throughout the night. Additionally, Mr. Dominic Martinelli, Chief of the Capitol Maintenance Department, will be assisting with the rescue effort."

"One last thing before I entertain questions," Simone remarked. "Dom will be the Designated Federal Official from eight p.m. until tomorrow at eight a.m. He will be on site throughout the night, and should there be any significant developments, we will text you. This allows other senior staff some much-needed rest. Okay, are there any questions?"

Several reporters were on their feet at once. Simone recognized Dave Dickerson with *USA Today* first.

"Ms. Perez, I recognize this is a very difficult situation. This crisis is now twelve hours old. Except for those individuals trapped in the café, we still don't know if there are any other casualties. Given all of this, why did you wait until now to bring in the team of engineers?" Simone opened her mouth to speak, but the reporter rushed on. "Additionally, what are Mr. Martinelli's specific qualifications to assume these responsibilities? For example, is he qualified to brief the Speaker if something unusual should happen?"

Simone took a deep breath, "Hindsight in these situations is always twenty-twenty. Do we wish we'd called in additional engineers sooner? Yes, of course. This is a fluid situation and I'd remind members of the press that all of the members of the interagency committee—and their staff—have been working around the clock since this incident occurred.

"As to Mr. Martinelli's qualifications—I'm rather surprised at the question. Mr. Martinelli—" The reporter tried to interrupt, but Simone continued smoothly. "Mr. Martinelli has served with distinction for thirty-six years. He has twice received the American Federation of Government Employees Employee of the Year award. Two former Speakers also recognized him for his outstanding service. Honestly, Dave, I really think Dom can handle this."

"One last question, Liz," said Simone.

"Liz Greybal with *The New York Daily News*." She looked down at her notes. "I know they were able to get insulin to Addie Hutchison, but I also understand she has other medical issues. Can you please tell us how she's doing and what will happen to her and the others in the café if they are unable to rescue them overnight?"

"It's my understanding that Addie Hutchison received the insulin and is feeling better. She does suffer from high blood pressure and this coupled with a badly broken shoulder is cause for concern. Our thoughts and prayers are with her and the others trapped in the café, as well as the fellows who are trapped in the mechanical room. We are doing everything we can to reach the café and will continue these rescue efforts throughout the night.

"Okay, thank you, that's a lid, everybody." Simone said. "Our next press briefing is tomorrow morning at ten a.m. See you then." Simone gathered up her notes as the reporters scrambled out the door.

As Joel reached for his satchel, he glanced over at Tyrone and noticed a single tear running down the boy's cheek.

༄

When Rob finally returned to the vent space at nine p.m. he was surprised to see Dom waiting for him. "Dom, what are you doing here? I had to take care of some personal business. I'd just assumed you'd called it a day and gone home."

"Well, I went to the office for a couple of hours. I came back because I figured you could use a hand. So, what's your game plan for this evening?"

Rob sighed and said, "Well, I'd really like to get to the mechanical room tonight. Thankfully, we're done with those stupid interagency meetings for today. And I suppose we should check on the folks in the café and say goodnight."

"Look," Dom continued, "why don't we skip making any radio contact with anyone until you make it through to the mechanical room? When we do make contact, let me do the talking. That way you can save your energy."

"Sounds like a plan to me. Give me about twenty-five more feet lead on my harness. It should make it easier to get to the mechanical room."

Rob quickly entered the now-familiar vent space and began worming his way toward the mechanical room. For some reason things seemed much easier tonight. He longed to shout out to the people in the café, but Dom was absolutely right: he needed to make it to the mechanical room tonight. When he came to an unexpected turn, he radioed, "Hey Dom, hang on to that harness; there's a turn up here I didn't expect."

"I've got your back, or in this case—your backside!"

They both laughed.

Rob made the turn with relative ease. At first, he heard nothing. As he inched his way forward, he thought he heard something. He stopped and listened intently. Nothing. As he resumed his efforts, another muffled cry broke the silence.

Again, the voice cried out. This time, Rob could make out the words. "Help! We're in the mechanical room. Please help us!"

"Dom, did you hear that?" Rob asked. He held his breath.

"I did," came the reply. Dom's voice was calm. "Just keep going at a safe pace. Remember, this isn't entirely up to you. Just take things slow and easy."

Rob leaned forward on his elbows and squirmed his way forward.

Finally, he lay above the mechanical room. As he looked down through the grate, he realized the explosion had drastically altered the ceiling of the mechanical room. He reached down and carefully pulled up the ceiling tiles. He smelled something rancid and he fervently hoped it was not the stench of death. As his eyes focused in the haze, Rob could see the blood-splattered walls and debris scattered throughout the room. He was horrified but managed to keep his composure. A large pipe lay across Billy's leg. Instantly, Rob knew this was the main steam pipe that ran heat from the mechanical room into the rest of the building.

He heard Fred cough.

"Billy? Fred? This is Rob. Are you guys okay?"

He tried to be as professional as possible, swallowing the lump in his throat.

"Rob, it's me, Fred." He labored for breath. "Fun day, huh? I'm okay, but Billy's hurt real bad. He's going in and out of consciousness. His leg is crushed!" Fred cried. "How soon can you get us out?"

As Rob tried to form the words, he heard Dom's voice. "Fred, this is Dom. The tunnel collapsed and there are search-and-rescue teams working throughout the night to rescue everybody. They're gonna want to know what Billy's blood type is. Can you ask him?"

Dom waited, listening. He could hear Fred trying to rouse his injured colleague. "He's A-positive," finally came Fred's voice.

"Okay, here's what I think Rob and I will do. We're going to do our darndest to get some food for you boys tonight. In fact, I'll try to get some-one to put something together and get back to you right away. It's important that Billy drinks, even if you have to wake him. He's gonna need fluid to make new blood.

"Look, I'm going to haul Rob out of here. We'll be back, I hope, within the hour," Dom said.

"Thanks, Dom," Fred said. "Rob, I'm so glad you're as skinny as a rail! Thank—" Fred tried to say more, but he succumbed to another bout of coughing.

Before Rob emerged from the vent space, Dom began ordering food and talking to emergency medical staff assigned to the rescue effort.

As Rob jumped down, Dom said, "Look, I hope you don't mind that I took over."

"Dom, to be blunt, this is the worst thing I've ever seen. Fred's awake, but Billy slips in and out. The main heating pipe fell across his right leg and . . ." Rob choked back a sob. "Oh God, Dom, its awful!"

"Let's try to get some food to them tonight. Hang in there! We'll find a way to get them out. I promise you, we'll get those boys to safety," Dom said. He patted Rob on the shoulder as he turned away.

Simone was bone-tired by the time she got home. She had intended to go straight to bed, but her cello beckoned to her from her living room, like an old friend whom she hadn't seen for far too long. A few minutes, she thought, just to take away the stress of this day. She carefully rosined up the bow and took the cello in her arms, as if in a lover's embrace. She slid her palm up the smooth neck of the instrument, her fingers deftly finding each note.

She began playing Bach's *Suite No. 1*, allowing the music to flow through her body. She remembered playing this piece at her high school graduation. The nuns even gave her extra time to practice, saying, "This is an important performance; you must do well."

How could she have known there would be a man at that performance from Juilliard Conservatory of Music who would offer her a full scholarship? She cried, but they were not tears of joy. For her, playing the cello represented very personal emotions. How could she explain the joy she felt when playing "Jesu, Joy of Man's Desiring," or the deep sorrow when playing Brahms's "Requiem?" In the end, she said no to the man from Juilliard and pursued an undergraduate degree in art history, in preparation for architecture school.

Simone continued to play and as she did, she thought about the people trapped in the café. She said a silent prayer for each of them and their families. She wondered how the two men in the mechanical room were and how soon they would receive medical attention.

Then her thoughts turned to John McIntyre, Speaker of the House. She wondered if there could be a chance that the two of them might fall in love and become a couple. "Those are silly, foolish thoughts, Simone," she chided herself. "He's way out of your league."

She finished playing, put her cello carefully back in its place, and went upstairs. As she prepared for bed, she noticed that her face was streaked with tears.

❧

By the time everyone in the café had something to eat they were ready to settle in for what would be a long night. Addie and Barbara sat at a table sipping tea while the men tried to put together makeshift bedding.

"Addie, tell me about yourself," said Barbara softly. "How did you meet your husband?"

"Well, my daddy owned a farm in southern Virginia—forty acres of tobacco. Sam came by with a buddy of his in an old beat-up truck. They had just gotten out of the Navy and lookin' to earn some extra money so that they could go on to Washington. Sam explained to Daddy that—on account of him being in the service—he planned to get a government job up in Washington. Well, Sam worked for Daddy six weeks and next thing I know, he's asking Daddy for my hand! We married and left. True to his word—Sam got a job at the Government Printing Office. It was a good job too."

"Wow, Addie, that's a lot of change all at once. Were you ever scared?" Barbara asked.

Addie shook her head. "No, I never felt scared. Sam was a good man with a deep faith. I knew for sure if he said he'd do something, well you'd best believe he'd do it. Like the house. He said he'd buy us a nice house and he did. He surprised me on our third anniversary. Before I knew it, Junior and Sissy were born. Once they went to school, well I came to work in Senate food service."

"So you went from motherhood to your career here?" Barbara asked.

"Well, you see, Sam got lung cancer. We had health insurance, but I needed to bring home the bacon, because Sam got so sick. He was diagnosed in May of '69 and died the following February. The kids took it hard. Junior was fifteen and Sissy was eight. Before I knew it, Junior turned eighteen.

"I come home one day, and he tells me he's enlisted in the Army—going to boot camp in a week with two of his buddies. Nothing I could do except talk to the Lord."

"Bet you did plenty of that! Oh, Addie; couldn't you talk sense into him?" Barbara cried.

"Oh, I tried. Men don't pay you no mind. I knew I'd lose that boy. Then eight months after he left, two Army guys in dress uniforms show up at my door. Didn't need to ask them why they were there. I knew. You know what? It was the one and only time I was glad my Sam wasn't here. There you are.

"But you know what? I am so grateful to God for the good times. There were many good times. How about you, Barbara? What's your story?" asked Addie.

"Well, I met Paul my first year in college. Paul was an upperclassman, funny, very outgoing. Well, I fell for him, and we married my sophomore year!" Barbara laughed, then continued. "Paul wanted to run for Congress from the very beginning. He never aspired to be the kind of flashy politician who's in it for himself. He genuinely wanted to help people. Six months after I married Paul, he started his first campaign for Congress."

"Of course, I had to play the role of loving, attentive spouse, which I rather enjoyed. I always enjoyed the campaign trail. Paul hated that part, but I connected with the voters. He really appreciated that. What I wasn't prepared for was the amount of entertaining which is expected of Congressional wives."

"Really? That must be tough!" exclaimed Addie

"Oh, Addie, you have no idea. It wasn't so much the entertaining in our home; I rather enjoyed that! There was some dinner or cocktail party every night. Of course, you still need to stay in touch with your husband's constituents back home. That's the one thing I do far differently from Paul. I think nothing of saying 'no' to plenty of invitations. I mean what are they going to do? If they vote me out of office, I'll return to our farm and live out my days in peace."

Addie smiled and said, "I never met Congressman Perkins, but I always heard good things about him. His staff always had good things to say about him, too. He had a real commitment to civil rights—for everybody."

"They were devastated when he was killed," Barbara said. "Fact is, it was tough the first few months, because here I am trying to help his staff grieve for him."

"Things are okay now?" asked Addie.

"Yes, they're much better." She smiled briskly and glanced at her watch. "Wow, we better stop talking and get some rest. I hope they can get us out of here sometime tomorrow morning." She laid a hand on Addie's hand. "Good night, Addie. Rest well."

"Good night, Barbara." Addie shook her head wearily and yawned. "God bless you."

10

DOM TOOK A DEEP breath. In his most authoritative voice he said, "Okay, I want everyone to listen up. We now have a Bobcat bulldozer which Reggie will be operating. If we all work together, I'm hoping we'll have the Senate side of the tunnel dug out by morning."

It was going to be a very long night and Dom had his hands full. He'd talked to Simone earlier in the evening to tell her they'd made it to the mechanical room and talked to Fred and Billy.

"They're in bad shape—but they're alive!" Dom had told her.

Simone had also asked that someone inform the Speaker of the latest developments, a task which Dom delegated to Rob.

He watched as Reggie carefully operated the Bobcat with a rhythmic motion—two feet in, dig in gently, two feet back. Two feet in, gently dig, two feet back. Scott stood parallel to the Bobcat, watching each move intently. The work was tedious and went on for over an hour without incident.

Then suddenly and unexpectedly Dom heard Scott yell, "Wait Reggie! STOP!"

In the harsh glare of floodlights, they saw an arm, then a leg, move.

Dom hurried from his perch just behind where Reggie was working, twenty feet forward. Eerily, a form roused itself from the rubble. A young man first sat up, then stood, coughing and trying to wipe dirt and dust from his face.

"Quick. Call medics. I need them in the tunnel RIGHT NOW," Dom yelled into his two-way radio.

The young man looked around, dazed, but somehow smiling. "I guess something happened, huh? I'm Ned Ramirez. I'm a House Page. I was going to the Senate documents room and wham, an explosion or something knocked me down. For a while it felt like I couldn't breathe. Then, I sorta cleared a little space—and waited. Guess I'll go get cleaned up."

Dom put a heavy hand on the boy's shoulder. "No! Wait, son. There was a very powerful explosion. You've been through a traumatic experience. We'll want to have you checked out by a doctor. Here's some water. Let me help you take off that neck tie."

"Sir," the boy protested, "The House will gavel in soon and I . . . '

"Young man, the Congress is in recess until further notice. I want you to stay here and be still. Let me see your arm. I'm no doctor, but I'll bet that's broken. Are you hungry?"

"Starved!" the youngster replied.

"Bring me a sandwich and a Coke, NOW!" barked Dom.

Before the medics arrived, Ned scarfed down two sandwiches and a Coke. When the medics arrived, Ned was asking if he could come back to help after he'd been checked out by the doctor.

"Thanks, son. But I have all the help I need," Dom replied. As the medics safely guided Ned toward an ambulance, Dom bellowed, "Reggie, Scott, let's get a move on, boys. Reggie, cut to the right eighteen inches. Good, now just keep doing what you were doing. Nice job, boys."

Then Dom gave a rare smile. Ned Ramirez was alive!

James and Jamal lay sleeping side by side on a couch. The two youngsters had eaten their second dinner in the large hearing room and had played with Mrs. Larson and Miss Amy until—finally—their older brother had put them down to sleep. Before tucking them in bed, all three boys had knelt and Tyrone prayed, "Dear Lord, this has been a weird day. Please be with Gran and help her not to feel any pain or to worry about us. Please bless all those trying to rescue Gran and all the others. In Jesus's precious Name"—and all three boys said, "amen."

Tyrone sat eight feet from them, at a small table staring intently at the screen of his laptop. He wanted to get this paragraph right. This was one assignment he would not blow. Finally, he wrote:

"The thesis of my paper will be that I support the First Amendment which guarantees freedom of the press. However, my paper will also show"—he deleted the word "show" and put the word "illustrate"—"that it is up to us citizens to demand better information—not someone's opinion. I believe the press should be free, but should give only accurate information in a timely manner."

Tyrone yawned as he read and reread the paragraph. He needed to provide at least five references—and he was just finishing up his list when Joel peeked in.

"Still at it, I see?" Joel asked in a hushed voice.

"Well, I'm not finished with my references yet, but I think I have my thesis. Want to see?" Tyrone clearly hoped for Joel's approval.

Joel read, then reread the paragraph before smiling, "Not bad. Not bad at all. So tell me, what did you think of the press conference? Did you like it or was it just plain boring?"

"Well, it made me wonder if that lady's hiding something. I mean, is Mr. Martinelli up to the job? And why didn't they call in more engineers right from the get-go?" Tyrone asked.

"I know Dom—he's very qualified. Dave knew better than to ask that question. Perhaps they should have hired more engineers sooner—gosh, I'm not sure it makes that much of a difference. This is a unique explosion and it's going to take a little more time.

"You see, sometimes the press needs to make a point. Sometimes we need to assume that those in charge—in this case Ms. Perez and Mr. Martinelli—know what they're doing. Your instincts are good! The key to any good journalist is to ask the right questions."

Joel yawned as he reread the paragraph. "So I was thinking, you're going to need to do more research on this paper. I mean it won't write itself, huh?"

Tyrone chuckled, "No, sir. This will take some time! I'll need to get myself to the library because we don't have internet at home. I just hope I can do a good job."

"So I was thinking," Joel said again, "What if you did a three month internship with me just while you write this paper? You could do much of your research and writing in my office. I'd expect you to come after school from three to six. Sometimes you'll run errands for me. Sometimes you'll do filing. Sometimes you'll sit in the press gallery and watch the House in action. You'd get a feel for how the press works."

Tyrone looked at Joel without speaking. Then he flashed a grin, "Wow, Mr. Joel, I'd love that! There's just two, okay three, problems with that. First off, I work hard in school and I get pretty good grades. I'm no scholar. To tell the truth, I really struggle with math. Second, my Gran probably wouldn't let me because she'd think my other schoolwork would suffer. Finally, Gran doesn't know this yet but I've already got a part-time job at night at the CVS. I'm tryin' to get some extra money to help with those two." He glanced over at his younger brothers.

"Well," Joel looked at Tyrone, "I'm not looking for some scholar. Heck, they're a dime a dozen around here. I'm just asking you to try it for three months. *The Washington Post* routinely sponsors high schoolers in these positions. I mentioned this very briefly to my boss and he says we could pay you one hundred fifty dollars a week, plus expenses. You seem to be interested in the press."

"Man, are you serious? *The Washington Post* would pay me to run errands? That sounds too good to be true." Tyrone looked at Joel with tears in his eyes. "I mean, I'd love to work for you. Maybe Gran will let me if you talk to her."

"I'll be glad to talk to her," said Joel. "You know, maybe we can work the hours out differently. Look, let's both keep thinking and talking. When Addie's feeling better, maybe the three of us can talk about it."

❧

Rob took a deep breath as he made his way to the Speaker's office. He was glad they'd been able to get some food and medicine to Fred and Billy before they took a rest break. Maybe everyone could sleep for a while.

Now all I have to do is update the Speaker, and then I can get some sleep.

When Rob arrived at the Speaker's office, the door was wide open but there was no one in the reception area. He knocked softly and said, "Hello, anyone home?"

In a moment, the Speaker's door opened and he said, "Rob! I'm glad you stopped by. Please, come into my office. Would you care for a soft drink?"

"No, sir, but thanks for the offer. I'm here because my boss, Dom, asked me to stop by and give you an update. We were able to get to the mechanical room and Dom wanted you to know the two maintenance staff—Fred and Billy—are alive and waiting to be rescued."

"That's wonderful!" the Speaker responded.

"Well, Billy's hurt pretty bad; his leg was crushed. Oh yeah, I almost forgot! Dom's crew just found the House Page alive! His name's Ned Ramirez and Dom thinks he's got a broken arm. Anyway, the kid's on his way to the hospital," Rob said.

"Wow, I'm delighted about the Page! Hopefully we can get those two fellas in the mechanical room to safety soon," John said. "By the way, I realized earlier this evening where I met you. A buddy of mine lives in Waldorf and we go fishing every few months. I went to the Friday night AA meeting—you sat toward the back—just like this evening," the Speaker said.

"Yes. I remember that meeting. Man, you do have a memory!" Rob said.

"So, Rob, you headed home to those three girls of yours?" John asked.

"I wish, but no. It's eleven-thirty now. Regulations require I take eight out of twenty-four hours off. I've got a couch reserved in Dom's office. I'm hoping to get back to work by six," Rob said.

"That's not eight hours!" the Speaker grinned. "You're standing here briefing me. That's work."

"Nope, you're wrong John," Rob said with a grin. "I am not briefing you. I am talking to a friend about my day. Good night, Mr. Speaker."

"Good night. See you tomorrow."

In the wee hours of the morning, two crews were working in the collapsed tunnel. The maintenance crew had managed to clear almost half of the debris and the team of engineers continued their arduous work.

Dom felt optimistic that if they could continue to make progress throughout the night they might reach the end by mid-morning. Then he heard one of the engineers shout, "Hold the phone! We have a huge problem!"

Dom rushed back to where the crew had been working and looked up where one of the young men shone a light.

"Mr. Martinelli, I'm Andy Taylor and I'm leading the team of engineers working on the tunnel. We've discovered what I think is a very serious problem. Look up and about forty-five degrees to the right. There's a huge fissure. We've been looking at this and we think it probably goes back about forty feet. Sir, I don't want to be an alarmist but if we're right—this could mean—"

Dom interrupted, "It could mean the entire structural integrity of the tunnel is not stable."

"Correct! We'd be putting everyone in the search-and-rescue effort in danger if we continue. In the morning I can call to get the equipment and supplies we'll need."

Dom stood silent for a long time, weighing his options. Then he asked, "How long will it take to confirm your suspicions? Assuming you're right, how soon can rescue efforts continue?"

"Mr. Martinelli, I really can't answer your questions right now; I wish I could. Let's assume the fissure is twenty-five feet long. We'll need to shore up the entire thing and under ideal circumstances, we'd do testing and . . ."

"First off, my name is Dom, okay? Just Dom! Second, these are not ideal circumstances. We have people to rescue. Some of them have serious medical problems. Their lives depend on us!" Dom sighed and continued. "Within the next three hours I want your team to put together a list of everything you'll need to fix this fissure. I'll get the equipment here as soon as I possibly can. It's two-thirty a.m. You fellas can go up to the cafeteria in the Rayburn Building; it's open all night. Please get the list to me no later than five-thirty. By six-thirty I expect everybody back on the job. Do you understand me? I'm asking you to condense five days of work into three hours. It's a herculean task. You guys up for it?"

Andy slowly nodded without speaking.

Dom added, "Here's my cellphone number. Call me if you have any questions. I'll let the engineers with Pickering know what's happened. I'll also call Simone Perez."

Then Andy and his crew of engineers trooped off to the cafeteria for food and coffee to fortify themselves for the most intense three hours of their careers.

11

LILLIAN HAWKINS ARRIVED MUCH earlier than usual Tuesday morning; seven-twenty to be exact. It surprised her to find the office empty, the door left wide open.

"Mr. Speaker?" she called out. When no one answered, she assumed John had slipped down to the gym to shower and change his clothes. Grateful for a few moments of quiet, Lillian put on a fresh pot of coffee. No sooner had the pot begun to brew than a clean-shaven Speaker of the House walked into his office.

"Good morning, Lillian. You're certainly here early!" John smiled at Lillian.

"How did you sleep, Mr. Speaker? Before you answer that question, I brought in some fresh banana bread and some oranges for breakfast."

"I slept fine. How did you get in so early and bring home-made bread? My goodness that smells wonderful!" John exclaimed.

"I had help. I mixed the batter last night. Vern baked it for me while I got ready for work. Then he surprised me by driving me in—without even being asked!" Lillian said, smiling.

As they were talking, Simone entered the outer office. Unsure of what to do, she finally called out, "Good morning!"

Lillian quickly got up and went to the reception area, "Good morning. How may I help you?"

Before Simone could answer, the Speaker came in and greeted her, still eating a slice of banana bread. "Simone, how are you this morning?"

"Fine, well until Dom woke me up at four-thirty. John, I'm afraid we have yet another problem to work through."

"Well, we'll figure it out. By the way, this is my Administrative Assistant, Lillian Hawkins. She is my guardian angel, to tell the truth. She came in early, bringing freshly baked banana bread still warm from the oven. I'll get you a piece. Grab some coffee and talk to me," John said.

Simone smiled at Lillian and said, "It's lovely to meet you. I have heard nothing but good things about you from several sources, including my own Administrative Assistant, Rita Muscelli!"

"That's right, Rita works for you. I'd forgotten that. Rita and I are in Toastmasters together. It's very nice to meet you, Ms. Perez," Lillian smiled.

"Please, I'm Simone. Before I leave, I'll give you my cellphone number. Today is going to be more difficult than yesterday, I'm afraid."

Simone poured herself a cup of coffee, walked in to the Speaker's inner office, and sat down. She took a sip of coffee and said, "At about two-thirty this morning, the team of engineers we hired yesterday alerted Dom to a fissure in the west half of the tunnel. Dom immediately took the workers out of harm's way. Everyone's okay, although one of the workers suffered a broken arm as a result of falling from the scaffolding."

John was listening intently.

"Dom woke me at four-thirty and I got here within an hour. Since I arrived, I've spent a good deal of time walking through the portions of the tunnel and talking to the engineers, trying to figure out a solution to this with Andy Taylor, the lead engineer. I'm torn. On the one hand, some very sick people are awaiting rescue . . ."

"And on the other hand," John said, finishing her thought, "we can ill-afford sending rescue teams into a part of the tunnel we know isn't structurally safe."

"Exactly! There's a meeting of the interagency workgroup at ten-thirty." Simone continued. "I'm hopeful they will come up with some solutions. Mr. Speaker—John—I've been an architect for twenty-three years. I taught at the university level for twenty years. Honestly, this is the most difficult structural problem I've ever encountered. Whatever solution we come up with, I must tell you there is no quick fix here."

"What are you saying, Simone?"

Simone hesitated for a moment, then said, "Although I am not going to announce this to the press yet, I'm terrified this rescue mission may take much longer than expected. I really hope I'm wrong." She looked down at her hands. "Perhaps someone else will have some other ideas. I've called some people from the American Institute of Architects, as well as the American Society of Civil Engineers. There may be some new technology or technique we can apply. This is an emerging situation." She shook her head. "I wish I had stayed here last night. Perhaps I could have somehow prevented this mess."

"You know as well as I do that this probably couldn't be prevented. Besides, you cannot work twenty-four/seven. I, for one, am glad you went home. As for the press, at some point we need to tell the press the truth. However, I agree for now, just give them the basics," John said.

Simone took a bite of banana bread and said, "I do have a small bit of good news for the press. The FINDER device—it allows us to detect victims trapped beneath the rubble—it only detected one person, whom we think is Ned Ramirez. Dom found him in the rubble last night."

"Yes, Rob told me! That's wonderful!" John exclaimed.

Simone nodded and continued, "I've moved the press conference up to nine-thirty. I plan to go straight to the interagency meeting to make introductions. I also want to make sure everyone works and plays well together."

John looked quickly at her. "Is there anyone in particular you're concerned about? And how is Dom faring?"

"I sent Dom off to sleep for a few hours. He'll be at the interagency meeting. As for my concerns, there is one person who I know for a fact will be an obstructionist," Simone said reluctantly.

"And that would be?" John asked.

Simone sighed. "Vaughn Hanesworth, with Pickering Architects, is an outstanding historic preservation architect. However . . ."

"However," John interrupted, "Vaughn Hanesworth is a pain in the fanny! I remember him lecturing me on the importance of preserving tile patterns in the House Cloak room. Tile patterns! As if the Founding Fathers explicitly picked them out as they passed around drafts of the Constitution!"

"So, you know what I'm up against," Simone said, rolling her eyes. "He's excellent at what he does. It's just that he can be so condescending," she finished.

"Why don't you remind him that I'm still Speaker of the House?" John said indignantly. "And that my highest priority is rescuing the people in the café and mechanical room. If Vaughn has a problem with that, let me know," John said insistently.

"I will, John. I will," Simone nodded.

"One more thing I must ask of you," John said, looking at Simone intently.

"What's that?" she looked up at him.

"Please don't knowingly put yourself in harm's way. Let the engineers do the crawling around."

"I can't promise you I won't spend a lot of my day in the tunnel. However, I won't take any unnecessary risks. I'll be in touch right after the interagency meeting. Thanks, John," she said, flashing him a smile as she rose to leave.

As she exited John's office, she handed Lillian a slip of paper. "Here's my cell number. And I must say, you make the best banana bread I've ever tasted! Please give me your recipe!"

"I'd be pleased to," Lillian said. "Feel free to call me—if I can help you today, I mean."

"I just may take you up on that."

As she walked toward her office, Simone realized it had been a long time since a man expressed any concern about her well-being.

Earl Bentsen took a deep breath and tried to collect his thoughts about what had happened last night. It was unbelievable! Earl had a difficult time knowing how to proceed. He knew he and Simone needed to present a united front if they had any hope of making progress today. He walked quickly through the halls of the Capitol, barely acknowledging anyone. He hoped he and Simone could have a few minutes to talk.

Earl found Simone in her office.

"Morning, Simone," he said hurriedly. "I trust you got some sleep last night. Can we chat?"

Simone looked up and replaced the phone receiver. "Earl! I was just calling to ask you to stop by. Do you want coffee?"

"Yes, thanks." He looked around and then sat down. Simone handed him a piping hot cup and he took several long sips before he said, "I'm glad to know no one else is trapped in the rubble. That said, I must tell you a thirty-four-foot fissure complicates this mission immeasurably! I'm figuring you're going to ask me for some bright ideas at the interagency committee meeting. I'm here to tell you I have very few ideas. Actually, I do have one . . ." His voice trailed off and he hesitated.

"What's your idea?" Simone asked.

"I'm hoping you and Dom will let me borrow Rob Tate for an hour or two. I need someone like him who knows the Capitol inside out and can think outside of the box. You remember my little spiel yesterday about only a limited amount of time to rescue folks?"

Simone nodded solemnly.

"I don't want to overstate my case, but we need other options. We have two guys in the mechanical room in critical condition. The fissure complicates everything. Let Rob and me see if there are some other rescue options. Perhaps we can find other ways of safely getting to the victims. I also had another idea, and I feel strongly about this," Earl added.

Simone nodded, "Go on Earl. I'm listening."

The Chief took a deep breath then said, "I think EMT Paula Winthrop should begin making some of the vent space runs, for two reasons. First, those boys in the mechanical room need medical attention. Billy has ongoing medical needs; receiving a blood transfusion is just the beginning. Second, Paula's thin, just like Rob. She's willing to traverse the crawlspace and that could take some of the pressure off Rob. If you agree with my assessment, would you please advise Dom? I don't want to get in the middle of the chain of command," Earl winked.

"I'll chat with Dom, but I'm positive he'll be fine with this plan. Besides, I was getting rather concerned about Rob. We also need Rob to help with some of the details of the fissure repair. Is Paula onboard with all this?" Simone asked.

"Oh yes, she's ready to go. One other thing."

"Sure. What do you need?"

"Please keep this quiet for the time being. I've done this a long time, and sometimes the press thinks we can work miracles, which of course we can't. I'd rather not share that Rob and I are looking for other options. I will be on site all day. I may have a few more fellas come over to help if Rob and I find something useful for them to do."

Simone nodded. "All of this is fine with me. I'd ask only that you attend the interagency meetings. You speak with authority, and clearly several of the committee members listen to you. Is there anyone else you need to take with you as you and Rob make your rounds?" Simone asked.

"Nope. Let's hope we can come up with some good answers. I need to check on some stuff. I'll be at the meeting. Then Rob and I can see if there's another way to skin this cat," said Earl rising to leave.

"Chief, thank you for coming to these meetings. By the way, it occurs to me you might need an office to crash in. Please make yourself at home," Simone said.

"Thanks. I'll take you up on that." Earl replied.

With that, Earl left.

Simone came into the briefing room sipping a latte. As the press conference began, she looked like a well-dressed professional, her bun firmly in place at the nape of her neck. Her tweed jacket and tan turtleneck signaled she was firmly in control. Yet, she felt overwhelmed and unsure of herself, hands trembling as she stepped to the podium.

"Good morning, everyone. Please take your seats as we have several new developments to make you aware of. Starting with the good news first. Rob Tate, who as you'll recall, is the fellow who's been crawling through the vent space, reached the mechanical room. We have confirmed the explosion originated with the new mechanical system. Two maintenance workers are alive and await rescue. One of the workers has a badly injured leg. As we speak, efforts are underway to get some blood to him.

"Turning now to the rescue efforts in the tunnel: I'm delighted to tell you Ned Ramirez, the House Page from New Mexico, emerged alive from the rubble late last night. His arm is broken and will require surgery. They are also giving him some sort of bronchial treatments since he breathed in rubble dust. Yet, according to Dom, the young man wanted to return and help with the rescue efforts. So hats off to Ned Ramirez! His parents, Elaine and William Ramirez, are en route to be with their son.

"I am also delighted to report that the FINDER device did not reveal the presence of anyone else. Of course, we still must rescue the two men in the mechanical room, as well as those trapped in the café.

"Now let me discuss the tunnel itself. I am sorry to tell you there have been some serious setbacks. In the early morning hours, our team of engineers discovered a rather large fissure in the tunnel. This is a very serious development. We have suspended all recovery efforts until further notice. Right now, a team of structural engineers and architects is trying to determine exactly how far this fissure extends and how we can best reinforce the tunnel so that rescue efforts may resume. One of the engineers will be at our next press briefing."

Simone paused as a member of the Speaker's staff handed her a note. She glanced down to read it and then looked up. "There will be a prayer service today at noon at the Washington National Cathedral for the victims of this disaster, as well as for the rescue efforts. I encourage you to cover that service. Okay, I'll take questions."

Chad Harris with the *New York Times* stood. "Ms. Perez, how will they transfuse the fellow in the mechanical room if they only have access to him from a fifteen-inch vent space? On another matter—you say a team of structural engineers is looking at the fissure. Can you tell us how this team was chosen and what their qualifications are to evaluate this problem?"

Simone nodded. "First, let me remind you that Pickering Architects, who are preeminent in historical restoration, were charged with making sure the Capitol building is structurally sound. Obviously, care must be taken, since the Capitol is an historic structure. This task may take several days. In order to help accelerate the search-and-rescue efforts, I hired a team of five engineers from Rockville Engineering Associates. They have been here since four o'clock yesterday afternoon. The team, led by Andy Taylor, identified the fissure at approximately two-thirty this morning."

Over a chorus of questions, Simone raised her voice.

"There will be a meeting of the Interagency Committee at ten-thirty. In addition, I've invited architects and engineers associated with the American Institute of Architecture. I hope they'll be able to help us make some wise decisions. It's impossible to know how long this will take. So, please understand that while it's important to resume the recovery efforts, we cannot risk having the tunnel collapse while the recovery effort is underway."

She continued.

"Regarding how they will facilitate a transfusion, EMT Paula Winthrop with D.C. Fire and Rescue will administer several units of blood in the very near future. Like Rob Tate, Paula is small and able to make it through the vent space. It's my understanding they plan to rig a rope ladder which will allow them to administer medications to the two victims."

Simone fielded several other questions before saying, "Ladies and gentlemen, I had planned to hold another briefing at one-thirty this afternoon. However, the Speaker has requested I accompany him to the National Cathedral service. Therefore the next press briefing will be at two-thirty instead. Thank you for understanding."

She gathered up her notes and stepped away.

❧

The café survivors were sitting at their tables in stunned silence.

As he ventured through the vent space, Rob Tate had spoken to the café via radio broadcast, "I'm sorry to tell you this. There's a temporary suspension in rescue efforts because the engineers found a huge crack in the tunnel."

There was silence from the café. Rob continued.

"We're not sure how soon rescue operations will resume. Please tell Addie that Miss Makayla has her boys. Well, it's a group effort—but the kids are in great hands."

Rob moved on, satisfied the café was informed.

Bruce Graham broke the silence. "This is government incompetence, plain and simple. When I get out of here I'm going to write a scathing letter to the Speaker demanding a complete and thorough investigation. This is unacceptable. I mean if I heard right, the fissure is at the House end of the tunnel. We're almost directly under the Rotunda. This is ridiculous!"

"Well, Bruce, they must not have any other options," Barbara said. "It sounds like the two fellows in the mechanical room are very seriously hurt. I'm just glad D.C. Fire and Rescue is able to minister to their needs. Speaking of which—how are you doing, Addie? You've been rather quiet."

"Well, I am so thankful my boys are all right!" Addie said with a grin. "I slept pretty well last night. My shoulder is fair—I mean it still hurts. If I don't move, I'm okay. But pretty soon I'm gonna need another insulin shot."

"Yes, you will," Barbara said as she considered breakfast options for Addie. "Addie, I know you're watching your cholesterol, but right now, I want you to have straight protein. No toast today. And I want all of you who've been hurt to have some Tylenol."

"Yeah, that's good," Addie said. "And after I eat, I'll have my devotions. Sorry the coffee's cold. Father Dan, you're awful quiet. Cat got your tongue?" Addie asked.

Dan tried to focus, but he saw double. His head throbbed. "Oh, Addie, I slept poorly, that's all. Once I get some Tylenol and some cold coffee, I'll be my old self."

He poured himself a cup of coffee and made it back to his seat. The room felt like it was spinning and the idea of eating anything was simply out of the question. *This will all go away*, he thought to himself.

"How about you, Jim? How are you feeling?" Barbara asked.

"Right now my only complaint is I'm missing my morning run! Other than that, I'm fine. I hope my wife is all right. Guess we have more time on our hands. After breakfast, let's start a gin rummy tournament!"

With that, the occupants of the café busied themselves, each one privately wondering when this ordeal might end.

12

SIMONE HURRIED THROUGH THE corridors of the Capitol, outside to the East entrance and down the steps to a limousine where the Speaker of the House sat waiting.

"John, I'm so very sorry to have kept you waiting. I was just speaking to the engineers and architects who are trying to decide the best way to fix the fissure in the tunnel."

"That's quite all right, I had Lillian Hawkins contact the Vicar of the Cathedral. He seemed delighted to have the extra time. Tell me, is there a consensus as to how to approach the giant crack in the tunnel yet? By the way, Lillian sent some coffee and a sandwich for you." John handed her a paper sack.

"There isn't a consensus, at least not yet," Simone replied. "There's a plan under discussion to reinforce the crack so it won't do any additional damage to the tunnel and then worry about the actual repairs to the tunnel later." She leaned back and took a sip of her coffee. "I must tell you that several of the engineers think that simply reinforcing the fissure could easily leave the whole structure more vulnerable. Vaughn Hanesworth is arguing against it. Of course, if we listened to Vaughn, we wouldn't clear the tunnel for another week!" Simone sighed and took a bite of sandwich.

"So, how are we going to make a decision?" John asked. He turned slightly to look at her intently, his blue eyes piercing her thoughts. "Like you, I'm concerned about so many aspects of this situation. My first priority is safely rescuing those trapped in the tunnel. Members on both sides of the aisle feel we're losing valuable floor time. I can hold them off—but not for long. You're the architect: What do you think?"

Simone looked at the Speaker and thought how at that very moment he looked childlike and vulnerable. "There are two things here. First, whatever else we may do, we must reinforce the fissure. That should take about twelve hours. Assuming that goes smoothly, I believe we should complete the search-and-recovery efforts. Then we can get to the more complicated matter of repairing the damage. Not everyone likes this two-pronged approach, including Vaughn. Let me text my staff to lean on the engineers. Hopefully, we can get consensus soon."

John nodded. "We must act quickly. Frankly, although I don't give a hang about what my members are saying, we cannot allow this to continue indefinitely. Too many lives are at stake. I'm looking to you to make certain this process moves along." He lifted an eyebrow.

"Understood," Simone said, smiling as she turned to the window. The limousine pulled up to the main entrance of the Washington National Cathedral. "Let me have a brief conversation with my staff, and I'll be in," Simone said.

The Speaker nodded, and they both stepped out as their aides opened the doors.

⌒

Makayla opened her eyes and turned off the alarm. The clock read: 1:00 p.m. She wished she could roll over and continue in blissful sleep, but that was not an option. Instead, she turned off the alarm clock, quickly showered, and put on a fresh U.S. Capitol Police uniform. She fixed herself a cup of instant coffee and poured a bowl of Cheerios. She wondered if the boys were okay and if Addie would be upset when she learned that her three grandsons would be missing a day of school.

Still, Makayla had no choice. She'd gone in to work yesterday at two-thirty p.m. and had worked a double shift—getting to bed at seven-twenty a.m. She turned on the news at WTOP and heard:

"I am standing outside the Capitol where we've just been informed that the search-and-rescue efforts have been suspended indefinitely while a team of engineers discusses how best to fix a giant fissure which has occurred inside the tunnel during the night . . ."

Makayla stopped eating and sat for a moment staring out her kitchen window. *Those boys are going to need some clean clothes—and a bath*, she thought. Then she realized her regular shift began in just over an hour. She gulped down her cereal, transferred her coffee to a travel mug, and headed for Addie's place to pick up clean clothes for the boys.

If she hurried, she'd be on time for the three p.m. roll call.

Colleen Larson sat lost in her own thoughts in the front row, with Amy at her side. Under any other circumstance, the Cathedral would soothe Colleen. She loved the soaring, majestic architecture and the details found in every corner of this edifice. It all pointed to something greater than herself. But not today. It had been thirty-six hours since Dan had left for Capitol Hill. Colleen knew Dan would be fine, yet she found it increasingly difficult to put up a good front. She even snapped at Amy when they'd gone home for a quick shower and a change of clothes.

As the organ began to play, she did not recognize the piece at first. After twenty-eight years of being married to a minister, a lot of sacred music began to sound alike. Then she recognized the melody, "Abide with Me". She struggled to keep her composure, as she used the kneeler, bowing her head, Colleen couldn't hold back her tears. How many times had Dan asked the organist to play this hymn at funerals? Even though she knew he'd be fine, somehow hearing this hymn right now left her needing her husband more than ever. When the hymn finished, the Speaker of the House made his way to the front of the Congressional delegation. Colleen made the sign of the cross and slipped again into the pew, carefully avoiding her daughter's gaze. She listened with head bowed as Father Stan Schulenburg began.

"We're gathered this afternoon to pray for everyone who has been impacted by the explosion which took place yesterday morning on Capitol Hill. I welcome each and every one of you to this service. We are particularly pleased to welcome those members of Congress who have joined us for this service."

Stan had been in the seminary with Dan, although they didn't know each other well. Still, he led the congregation deftly, taking care to be as optimistic as possible. At the end of the service Stan said, "And I pray for the safe return of my brother in Christ, Father Dan Larson, who's the Rector of Saint Matthew's Episcopal Church.

After the service had concluded, Colleen thanked Stan for his kind words. Then she quickly left the cathedral, grateful to reach the anonymity of the family car.

Rob walked the halls with Chief Bentsen, looking for some sort of workable solution to this crisis. As they walked, Earl peppered Rob with a million questions. Were there any other old dumbwaiters in the building? Had there been any significant duct work done in the recent past? *He definitely knows his stuff*, thought Rob admiringly. He knew the Chief wanted to find other rescue options. Still, Earl Bentsen took his time, carefully surveying his surroundings.

When they reached the second floor, Earl asked, "Tell me, any chance there could have been another cavity in the building? I don't know, maybe a janitor's closet or an old elevator shaft? I know it's a longshot."

Rob froze for a long moment. He remembered an old elevator that they took out right after he was hired. Excitedly, he turned to the Chief and said, "Come with me. This won't be in the blueprints Simone and Dom are poring over. I don't know who's in the office now, but we did take out an elevator in order to expand some Congressman's office. He had a disability and had requested a private, accessible restroom. I helped take the elevator out. I was still wet behind the ears. Why didn't I think of this before?"

"Relax, Rob; you can't think of everything."

They finally reached the room. As they walked in, Rob showed his badge.

"Hi, I'm Rob Tate with the Maintenance Department. This is Chief Earl Bentsen with D.C. Fire and Rescue. If my memory serves me correctly, there's an accessible bathroom in this suite, right?"

The young man behind the reception desk looked up and managed a tentative "Yes." He looked at them curiously. "Why do you want to know?"

The Chief spoke up, "We're trying to find alternative ways to rescue the two gentlemen who are trapped in the mechanical room. There's a chance there may have been an elevator shaft below the bathroom. That would greatly increase our chances of getting to them. Could you ask your boss if Rob and I could take a peek?"

"Sure."

Within minutes a woman—clearly a senior official—came out and simply said. "Guys, you do whatever you need to rescue those boys. Want a soda or something?"

"Nope, just like to look at the bathroom," Rob said, "Oh, and thanks a ton."

As soon as they were inside the bathroom, Rob's hunch paid off. The tiles didn't match. Rather, they could clearly see that the old tile had been there for a very long time. There was also a swath of newer tile—about eight feet in diameter—just about the size of an old elevator shaft. Rob's excitement dissipated with Earl's quizzical look. The Chief was obviously thinking this through.

"Tell you what," Rob said, getting to his feet, "let's go one floor down and see what's what." Earl nodded. "We'll be back in a bit," Rob said to the young man as they made their way out of the office.

What they found on the first floor left them speechless for several moments. There, in the middle of a typing pool, sat a huge closet. Rob got the door open, looked inside and confirmed it had once been an elevator.

"Here's the problem," he said to Earl, peering up inside. "This elevator shaft is about six to ten feet from the mechanical room. How in the world are we going to get those guys that far?"

"Rob, that's not a problem," Earl assured him. "Heck, most of our rescues require some sort of transport. Let's go find Simone and Dom. I think we just caught a break!"

⌒

"Good afternoon. This is the Speaker's Office. How may I help you?"

Lillian prided herself on polite and accurate telephone protocol.

"Hello. This is Congresswoman Janine Albright. Who am I speaking to please?"

"Hello, Congresswoman Albright. This is Lillian Hawkins. I am the Speaker's administrative assistant. How may I help you today?"

"Hello, Lillian. Is the Speaker available by any chance?" Lillian sensed the young woman had been crying.

"I'm sorry, Congresswoman Albright. The Speaker is at a prayer service at the National Cathedral today for the victims of the explosion. I don't expect him back until three-thirty, or perhaps later. May I have him call you when he returns?"

"Well, I really need to speak to him today." With that, the Congresswoman lost her composure and sobbed uncontrollably for several moments. Once she regained her composure she said, "I have a very personal matter to talk to John about. Do you happen to know what time he'll be leaving this evening? I'd like our meeting to be—discreet."

"The Speaker will probably be here very late into the evening. He wants to be supportive of the rescue crews." Lillian knew the Speaker planned to stay all night again. Nevertheless, she saw no reason to share this information with the entire House of Representatives.

"Could you tell him I'll stop by at eight o'clock this evening? Hopefully no one else will be around."

"That's fine," Lillian assured her. "I'll make certain he's aware you're coming to speak to him privately. One more thing; I will be ordering some dinner for the Speaker. May I get something for you as well? You sound like you're having a tough day," she said.

There was silence for a moment, and then the Congresswoman said softly, "You are very kind. I have dinner plans. Nevertheless, thank you very much. I'll be there at 8:00."

With that, the Congresswoman hung up.

Simone stood at the head of the long conference table and cleared her throat. "Ladies and gentlemen, as all of you know, we've discovered a fissure in the tunnel. It's at least forty-five feet long and poses a real threat to the structural integrity of the tunnel. This complicates our rescue efforts. The focus of this meeting is how to repair this fissure. This is going to be a difficult discussion, but I'd ask each of you to be candid with your concerns."

As Simone spoke, Chief Bentsen came in.

"Chief Bentsen, glad you could join us," Simone called out. "Come on up. I'd like your thoughts about where things stand."

"Simone, we find ourselves in a real fix," Chief Bentsen said as he stepped up to the table. "I'm very reluctant to stop all search-and-rescue efforts, but we have no choice. I am inclined to allow the team of engineers to fix the fissure. I will say this: D.C. Fire and Rescue stands ready to assist in any way possible. If you have work which requires engineers, I can't help you. If you have work that simply needs some brawn to get the job done, I have fifteen young cadets just hanging around my firehouse waiting for a call.

"I am hopeful, however," he continued, over a gentle ripple of laughter, "that we may have found an alternative solution which will help us get to the victims sooner. Rob Tate and I just combed the Capitol and it seems one of the members years ago needed an accessible restroom. Turns out the restroom used to be part of an elevator shaft which exits into the hallway about ten feet away from the mechanical room."

There were audible sounds of relief and muted applause.

"Let's not get ahead of ourselves," cautioned Earl. "I have some research to do yet. However, I think it may work. It is imperative everyone keep this under your hat! If the press get wind of this, they'll hound Simone and me night and day! Also, if anyone has any other ideas, please let me know. Nothing—and I mean nothing—should be off the table."

Earl sat down, looking weary.

"Thanks, Chief," Simone said. "I must underscore Earl's remarks and ask each of you to keep that information to yourselves, until we have this alternative scoped out. I'd hate for our friends in the press to get their knickers in a knot for nothing."

Simone took a deep breath as several people began to speak at once. She raised her voice.

"Ladies and gentlemen, please, we must respect each other. I want Captain Dupre to weigh in. Paul, what are your thoughts on how we should deal with this fissure? Specifically, does the fissure affect security?"

Paul Dupre leaned forward and said, "I'm not particularly concerned about the fissure's impact on security. Public safety is my primary concern. I'll place extra guards around the perimeter of the fissure. Frankly, the press is everywhere and folks are wandering around where they absolutely shouldn't be."

He paused and looked around the table.

"If any of your workers sees a civilian in the tunnel, please radio me immediately. This is one situation where the phrase 'if you see something, say something' applies. My role in this mess is to keep everyone safe and to back up the Chief in any way I can."

"Thanks, Paul, that's very helpful," Simone said and continued, "I want to call on Andy Tylor who will be representing the team of engineers working on the fissure. Andy, what do you have in mind?"

"Thank you, Ms. Perez. I have been on-site all morning and this fissure is actually much worse than we originally thought. My team and I will be working to replace the struts and reinforce those places which are the most vulnerable to further rupture. Of course, we'll be working closely with Pickering Architects to ensure the historical nature of the tunnel remains intact. I must ask that no other work be done in the tunnel until we've completed this task."

"Why is that Mr. Taylor?" Earl asked.

"Chief, it's our assessment that the tunnel is just too fragile. My concern is it could further rupture, and no one wants that to happen."

Simone spoke up, "Andy, how long will it take you and your team to complete this work? And what help will you need?"

"That's difficult to say. I'm concerned about giving a specific time for completing our work."

The Chief's frustration began to boil over. "Young man, I understand your team is in an unenviable position. Still, I must remind everyone that there are people who need rescuing. At least two of these folks have life-threatening problems. I understand the bind you're in, believe me, but I must ask for regular updates in order for us to understand what's going on."

He sat back, a flush of anger coloring his cheeks.

Simone stepped in and said, "Okay, here's what we'll do. I'll be working with Andy throughout the night. I'll send out texts every two to six hours. If anyone has questions, by all means, please let me know. Looking directly at Vaughn Hanesworth she asked, "Will you be representing Pickering tonight? I ask because I think it's important, given the fragility of the situation."

"I suppose so, although I don't see that it is necessary. Once again, Ms. Perez, you miss the point."

Simone leapt to her feet. She looked at Vaughn without blinking and said steadily, "You will not speak to me like that. You have questioned my competence from the beginning. If you don't intend to fulfill your contractual obligations, that's up to you. However, I'll not allow you to question my judgment."

"We are done here. Everyone, its four p.m. now and I am holding a press briefing at five-thirty. I do not feel there is a need to reconvene our working group again today. However, I am asking that representatives from the Maintenance Department, D.C. Fire and Rescue, Pickering Architects, and the team of engineers be present throughout the night. Please watch for a text from me making these arrangements final.

"Let's meet here tomorrow morning at eight a.m. sharp."

13

COLLEEN STOOD IN HER kitchen, stirring spaghetti sauce and making a large salad. With rescue efforts temporarily suspended, the Architect of the Capitol encouraged family members to go home and get some rest. It seemed to Colleen that this waiting could go on indefinitely. After consulting with Makayla, they had decided James and Jamal would go to the Larson home for the night. Colleen planned to drive them to school in the morning. Tyrone had accepted Joel's invitation to come to his basement apartment and work on his paper.

James and Jamal raced downstairs clad in their pajamas, fresh from a hot bath. "Man, something sure smells good. I'm hungry!" James said.

"We're supposed to ask how we can help. At home we set the table." Jamal said, seeming pleased with himself.

"Well, that would be very nice, Jamal," Colleen said, smiling. "The silverware is in the drawer right over there. I'll have Amy get the plates down. Do you guys have any homework? Tomorrow is a school day, you know," Colleen asked.

The two boys looked at each other, not knowing what to say. "Well, see, since we didn't go to school today, we don't know for sure if there is any homework. Besides, we're pretty worried about Gran," Jamal added.

Amy had taken a quick shower and came downstairs, dressed in her robe and Mickey Mouse slippers. "Guys, I think you both have books in your knapsacks. How about after we eat, you two curl up and read? We all need some extra sleep tonight."

"Can we watch TV?" James asked.

"After you read, we'll see." Colleen dished steaming pasta into a bowl. She reached into the oven and the smell of hot garlic bread wafted through the kitchen. "Dinner is served, gentlemen!"

As everyone gathered at the kitchen table, Colleen turned to Amy, "Honey, please say the blessing."

Amy made the sign of the cross and simply said, "God, we are grateful for these boys and for a night at home. Please watch over Daddy, and Addie, and the others trapped in the tunnel. Please be with the rescue team, for Jesus' sake, Amen."

They ate quietly, with even the boys too tired for conversation.

By eight p.m., Colleen tucked everyone in for the night.

Simone sat at her desk, trying to return some calls.

"Yes, I understand, Madam Chair. You must understand that I felt we had no other choice. I will have architects here twenty-four/seven and I give you my word that as soon as the survivors are safely rescued, we will commence with a thorough assessment of the structural integrity. It's very likely that the tunnel will remain off limits to the public for weeks, if not months."

She finished the conversation as Dom walked in, a grin on his face.

"Dinner is served. Best Philly cheesesteaks in town! I also bought two Cokes."

They began devouring the meal.

"Oh, Dom. This is the best thing I've eaten in months. Where did you get these?"

"I know this little hole-in-the-wall over on New York Avenue. I hope you don't mind hot peppers." He gave her a sheepish grin.

"Are you kidding me? My motto is 'The hotter the better.' So, Dom, after you eat I want you to go home. Tonight's my turn to play 'senior staff.' I am, after all, the Architect of the Capitol," Simone chuckled.

"Simone, you might be my boss, but I am your senior by about twenty years. If you want to stay tonight, that's your decision. However, I am not going home tonight. There's just too much going on. By the way, I took a three-hour nap while you were at the Cathedral. If you agree, I might not even need to come in tomorrow." Dom said, grinning.

Simone wiped mayonnaise from the corner of her mouth, then asked, "Tell me, does your wife ever win an argument?"

"Sometimes. She's Sicilian: they're hotheads!" Dom laughed.

"How many of your staff will stay tonight? I am specifically concerned about Rob Tate. Has he been home yet?" asked Simone.

"No. He wants to stay. Paula Winthrop will go off duty at eight after she delivers another dose of insulin to Addie. I want to save Rob for other assignments."

"I agree completely. If Rob had just a little more experience . . ." Simone's voice trailed off, but Dom sensed her thoughts.

"He'd make a great replacement for me. He just doesn't have the administrative experience yet. Still, Rob knows more about the Capitol than anybody and will make a fabulous assistant director. I'm not telling you what to do or anything."

Simone looked up without expression and said, "So let me recap: we're both staying all night, Rob is the best, and I've found out where I can get a decent steak sub."

"That sums it all up. There's one last thing," said Dom with a mischievous grin. "How come it took this tragedy for us to, well, become friends?"

"We're both very obstinate people and used to getting our own way. Look, I need to run. Thanks for supper." She said, handing him a twenty. Then Simone added, "One last thing. If Rob—or any of your staff—is too tired to drive, but wants to go home: call this number. The Speaker has authorized the use of his limousine service."

❧

John McIntyre's exhaustion finally caught up with him. On any other night, he would have simply packed his briefcase and headed home. The tunnel's safety remained in question, occupants of the café needed rescuing, and the fellows in the mechanical room needed medical attention. The explosion remained John's biggest concern. Still, myriad other matters demanded his attention. The House budget process had degenerated into a free-for-all. The scheduled debate on the DOD appropriations legislation had fallen woefully behind. The House Education and Labor Committee had major concerns about the Administration's appointees to the Civil Rights Commission. All of these matters required his attention. John heard a gentle knock on his door and fervently hoped it was Simone.

"Hello, Mr. Speaker?" Congresswoman Albright called out.

John poked his head through the door and smiled. "Janine! It's nice to see you this evening. Lillian said you'd be stopping by. Please, come in and sit."

"May I shut the door?" Congresswoman Albright asked.

"It's really not necessary. Everyone's left for the day." John said.

"I have a very personal matter to discuss. I'd be far more comfortable if your office door is shut." She closed it without awaiting the Speaker's reply.

John instinctively smelled trouble. "What's the matter? You've been crying; I have two daughters, so I can tell. Talk to me."

Janine Albright had represented the 12th District of California for two terms. In her early thirties, Janine's attractive appearance, coupled with her political pragmatism, enabled her to get things done. She eagerly took on new assignments and always kept the Speaker apprised of new developments. Her skills portended a nearly perfect Representative.

"I don't really know how to begin this conversation. I've made a complete mess of my life. Let me start by telling you the facts: I'm two months pregnant—"

"That's wonderful! "John interrupted, somewhat bewildered. "Todd must be thrilled. What, are you needing extra time for maternity leave?'

"You don't understand: this is not Todd's child. I've fallen in love with Chris Spencer. He's a legislative assistant to Congressman Mark Schloss. John, I know you're a man of high moral principles. I also know you're fond of Todd, so you should know we're married in name only. We somehow grew apart. Now I don't know what to do. I only know two things. I'm in love with Chris Spencer and *The Washington Post* is breaking this story tomorrow. A reporter named Greg Long wrote the story."

Janine buried her head in her hands and sobbed.

John mused as to how to help her; Janine Albright and his oldest daughter were about the same age. He felt so bad for this young woman, although she'd obviously made some poor choices.

"What should I do? I guess my political career is over. Most voters would be thrilled if I announced this pregnancy, but not many will be thrilled when I mention I'm not married to the father. Abortion is not on the table, I could not do that. I haven't told Chris yet. We're meeting for dinner in an hour."

Janine's eyes were red, and she looked exhausted.

"Janine, I can call *The Post* in a few minutes. The editor owes me a couple favors. I'll ask him to sit on this story for a week. I encourage you to fly home in the morning. Talk with Todd. Make certain your feelings for him are completely over. Marriage is a very tough thing sometimes. I know; I was married to my late wife for thirty-two years. Once you and Todd are in agreement—even if that agreement is divorce—then we can talk about your political future. Chris Spencer won't like me very much, but that's okay. He's a bright young man."

John dialed a number from a small book he kept in his breast pocket. On the third ring someone answered, "*The Washington Post.*"

"Good evening, this is John McIntyre. Is George Grady there please?"

"Mr. Speaker, sir," a staff person stammered. "Yes, just one moment."

"John, you old dog. How are you?" George asked as he came on the line.

"I'm just fine, George, although this week has certainly been one for the books. Listen, I am calling up a favor. A reporter named Greg Long wrote a story he's planning to run in tomorrow's *Post* about Congress-woman Albright," John said.

"Yes, that's right. Front page—just below the fold. She's a member of Congress and her pregnancy's fair game, especially given the circumstances."

"Sit on it, George. I'm asking you as an old friend. I haven't called in a favor from you in a long time," John said simply.

"How long are we talking, John? I mean, the public has a right to know," George insisted.

"Not before her constituents—or for that matter, her husband," John retorted.

"How long? *The Post* editorial board won't wait forever."

"One week." He paused. There was silence on the other end. "Please, George. I'd be really grateful."

George sighed. "All right, one week. In return, I want an exclusive in-terview with you after the tunnel's clear."

"You've got it. I'll throw in a steak dinner. Thanks for your help. Please remember me to Zelda."

John hung up the phone and turned to Janine.

"Congresswoman, please take some time to think carefully about your situation. I'm not worried about your political career, although it's going to be rough sledding for a while. I have every confidence in your professional skills. However, as a friend I'm deeply concerned about your emotional well-being. Perhaps you have a trusted confidant or a pastor back home. Talk to that person. Don't make this decision on a whim. I'd hate to see you make a decision you may regret later."

Janine sat, looking at her knotted hands. Then she said in a strained voice, "Mr. Speaker, your kindness is astounding. I came here thinking you'd ream me out. Instead, you're helping me think this through. I still have some really deep feelings for Todd. Now I'm expecting another man's child. You want to know the real irony? Todd would be thrilled if I were pregnant with his child." She blinked back the tears. "Thank you very much for your kindness." She stood to leave.

"Please stay in touch; call me next week, okay?" John said.

"If you're not here, who should I leave a message with?" Janine asked.

"Ask for Lillian. In case you're worried, Lillian can keep confidences. Trust me on this. She knows some things about my daughters they won't even tell me!"

✑

Tyrone lay sprawled out on an overstuffed couch, staring at his computer. Next to him, Joel read a science fiction novel, grateful for a few quiet hours. They'd opted for Chinese carry-out and their empty cartons lay strewn around the living room. Joel sipped a beer, and considered offering one to Tyrone, but thought better of it.

Tyrone broke the silence. "So, is CNN a news station or just another reality TV show? I mean, I really do support a free and independent press. My problem is, what exactly is the free press? Right now, I'm too tired to figure it out."

"Man, I know what you mean," Joel said, laying down his book. "I turned in the shortest article in my entire career today. I basically said, not much has changed—more news as it breaks," Joel said.

"But won't that get you in trouble? I mean your boss—what will he say?" Tyrone seemed a bit perplexed.

Joel laughed. "Tyrone, I'm exaggerating. I gave them all the facts. Most of the facts weren't new. Besides, Harry would let me know if he had a problem with my writing. It's on the website, so I'm good. How about you? I think you've got a lot on your plate. Forgive me if this is too personal but . . . you got a girlfriend?"

Tyrone laughed and said, "No, sir. Not now. I've got to take care of these boys. Someday I'll go after a girl. I mean there's one at church, but I don't have the time or money. I gather there's a woman you like . . . a whole lot."

They both laughed.

"Yes, it's true. Actually, I should have told you this sooner. Congresswoman Barbara Perkins is my girlfriend. I'm hoping to make her my wife. But that's between us, okay?"

Tyrone smiled at Joel and said, "Don't worry, Mr. Joel, your secret's safe with me."

"Grab your jacket. Let's go," Joel commanded.

"What for? Where?" Tyrone jumped to his feet.

"I want you to meet the other love of my life."

At first, Tyrone thought they were going to a bar to meet some woman. He was even more confused when Joel headed for his backyard. There, under a worn canvas tarp, appeared the most beautiful thing Tyrone had ever seen: a Harley-Davidson Low-rider. It sat there gleaming in the light from the porch, just waiting for Joel to kick her into life. Joel handed Tyrone a helmet and said: "Never—and I mean never—take a baby out without a helmet."

They walked the bike out to the street. Joel swung onto it and said: "Hang on to me. When I lean into a turn—stay with me. This is my other baby."

They rumbled slowly down the street, paused briefly at the stop sign, and then roared out to Highway 295, over the Wilson Bridge and past the Lincoln Memorial. For a blessed hour they forgot about the explosion, about Addie and Barbara—about everything. Tyrone still didn't know what to think about falling in love with a girl. Nevertheless, that night began what would become a life-long affair with Harley-Davidson motorcycles.

∾

Simone sat at her desk working on some calculations. Soon, it would be her turn to work on the installation of the struts in order to fix the fissure down in the tunnel. Her calculations had to be exact: lives depended on it. As she worked, classical music came from her cellphone on her desk. Vivaldi's "Water Music" played softly. It soothed her soul. The music enabled her to focus on her calculations, pouring all of her energies into the task at hand.

The Speaker knocked softly, but Simone did not hear him, continuing to work intently.

John finally cleared his throat and said, "Simone, can you take a break? You're working awfully hard there."

"John. How are you doing? I'm getting ready to go help install the struts. My shift starts very soon. I'm hoping we can work quickly."

"Have you had dinner yet?" John asked, trying to be nonchalant.

"I had a dinner meeting of sorts with Dom. You haven't had your supper yet? Goodness. I have half of my steak sub left over from dinner. I must tell you it's the best sub I've had in years. Let me get it for you and we'll visit while you eat." Simone saved her calculations and quickly retrieved the sub and a Coke. "How come you're eating so late? You must be famished." Simone said as she placed the food in front of him. "By the way, you may want to take some of the hot pepper off."

Simone's advice came too late. John's eyes watered and he took a long drink of Coke. "My goodness, this is hot all right." He opened the sandwich and tried to scrape off the red peppers.

"Sorry. Dom and I both like things hot."

"Now that I got some of the hot stuff off, it's good. I'd planned to eat about eight, but a member of Congress called with a personal problem and needed my help. It happens," John said.

"My two-hour shift begins as soon as I can get there so I'd better get a move on," Simone said. "I'll try to stop by later in the evening, but I make no promises."

"No, please stop by. When are you going to sleep?" John responded.

"I slept last night. Besides, sleep is highly overrated; a lesson I learned in architecture school. See you later."

"Bye now," John smiled as he left her office.

෴

Sometime during the night, Billy awoke from a beautiful dream. He and his fiancée, Beth, were married and on some island resort for their honeymoon. Everything felt perfect and he wanted it to go on forever. After waking, it took Billy a few moments to remember where he was. He really didn't care. All he wanted was to hold Beth and feel the cool sea breeze against his skin. Then a sharp jab of pain jolted him fully awake. He realized he was still in the mechanical room.

The morphine has finally worn off. Who knows how long it'll be before that nurse comes back?

He cursed himself for not waiting for the Capitol Power Plant guys to come on-site. He could find no comfort. He wanted to call out to Fred and wake him up. Fred slept deeply, oblivious to his surroundings. Billy found himself needing some companionship through the long night. He wanted to move the pipe that trapped his left leg.

I'm a strong guy. Heck, I can bench press two hundred and thirty pounds at the gym.

He tried again, pressing harder. He felt weak. Finally, reluctantly, he realized it was no use. He cursed in the night and lay back, exhausted. After a very long time, just as he was on the cusp of sleep, Billy heard his grandmother singing, *"Jesus loves me, this I know."*

His beloved grandmother had been dead for ten years.

14

BARBARA WOKE UP FIRST, in a dreamlike state. She opened her eyes and lay still in the pitch black. She knew something was very wrong. She prayed silently, "Oh, dear God, please let this be only a bad dream. Bless those who seek to rescue all of us. And please comfort Joel until we are together again."

Before she could whisper "Amen," she heard what sounded like a loud clap of thunder—except it was very clearly inside the building. Now everyone began to stir.

"What the . . . ?" Bruce grumbled.

They all began to speak at once, but Jim demanded silence. "Be quiet and let me listen!" When he finally spoke, Jim said ominously, "Guys, something just happened. I don't know what—but I'm pretty sure it's not good."

"We don't know that," Father Dan broke in. "For all we know, there's a simple explanation for what we just heard. We just need to have faith that . . ."

"Please, Father, enlighten us," Bruce said, mockingly. "You and Addie sit here praying and reading your Bibles or prayer books or whatever. Nothing happens. Nothing. That's the problem with you religious people—you never have any plausible explanations."

Addie sat up straight. "As I said before, I will have none of this sort of talk. Mr. Bruce, shut your mouth. We don't sit in judgment of you, so don't you go passing your judgments on us," Addie said, bristling. "Now let's try to get some more sleep. There's nothing we can do about whatever happened."

Everyone tried to go back to sleep—except Barbara. She lay in the dark, listening with all her might. Listening and thinking about how much she missed Joel.

༄

Dom gently shook Simone's shoulder. "Simone, you gotta wake up. There's a big problem."

She jerked awake and sat up at her desk, rubbing her eyes. "What's happened? What's wrong?"

"There's been an accident," Dom said cautiously. "Unfortunately, we were wrong about the stability of the tunnel infrastructure. The engineering team was installing the struts, as planned. Apparently some of the coordinates were miscalculated and . . . well, the tunnel imploded. We need your input before we can go any further. I didn't know what else to do."

Simone blinked. "So the situation is worse now than it was before?"

"Simone," Dom said, struggling to maintain his composure, "I want you to know, we did the best we could—we really did. We couldn't avoid what happened. Please come with me. Andy will explain the whole situation."

They walked in silence out of her office.

"How bad is it?" Simone asked, as they made their way to the tunnel. "Can we still get through to the café by tomorrow morning?"

Dom did not answer. Rather, he said brusquely, "Put on your hard hat. This is a dangerous situation."

When they arrived, Andy struggled to look Simone in the eye. He said, "Okay, here's exactly what happened. Dom came to me about two hours before this happened and said he thought someone may have miscalculated the torque needed on the struts. I'm a civil engineer and so, to be honest, I'm not paying Dom much attention. As it turned out—Dom had it right. The pitch on the struts was much too steep and it caused the tunnel to partially collapse." He looked away for a moment and then continued, "When this happened, three-quarters of the tunnel imploded. We are, for all intents and purposes, back to square one."

"Take me there. I need to see this for myself. Are there any fatalities?" Simone demanded.

"No, everyone got out safely. One of Earl Bentsen's cadets fell from the scaffolding and broke his ankle, but he'll be fine. However, most of the progress we've made over the last eighteen hours is gone."

As they walked, Simone attempted to pull herself together. She'd have to wake the Speaker soon—very soon. Her mind flicked over the questions that were flooding in. She glanced sharply at Andy. "Where was Vaughn Hanesworth during all this?" Her jaw clenched. "When I left my shift at eleven, I had the clear understanding that he'd be on-site throughout the night. What happened?"

Andy did not answer right away but finally mumbled, "Mr. Hanesworth went home . . . at eleven-thirty."

"Who calculated, or shall I say miscalculated, the coordinates for the struts?" she demanded.

"Mr. Hanesworth," Dom said. "He did the calculations very quickly. He insisted that anyone could do them. I was very skeptical. What could I say? He's my senior in this operation."

She didn't try to contain her anger. Instead, she pulled out her cellphone and punched Vaughn's home number. Andy and Dom looked at each other. His wife answered, none too happy with this call. "Please let me speak to Vaughn."

"He's sleeping right now."

"Wake him up." When he finally answered, Simone said emphatically, "Vaughn, you get yourself in my office within the next hour or I can absolutely guarantee the front page of the morning edition of *The Washington Post* will read, 'Pickering Architects to be sued for professional malpractice by the Architect of the Capitol!'" Simone hung up.

Finally, they reached the collapsed portion of the tunnel. All of the progress accomplished over the last two days lay in ruins. Simone could not have imagined the devastation. She stood there speechless, fighting back tears. The tunnel had almost fully collapsed on the north side.

As she took it in, Dom looked at Simone and said, "I'm so sorry. I should have been able to prevent this. I feel like I've let you down."

"Dom, there is only one person who's let me down—let us all down—and that's Vaughn. I will deal with him directly and he will not like what I have to say. I do not in any way hold you responsible."

Then she turned to Andy and asked: "How quickly can you get additional staff down here? We've got to get this search-and-rescue completed. I want you to look at every option. We'll need a crane." She looked him in the eye. "We have to complete this mission: lives are at stake. I want your secretary—or whoever—to keep detailed records of what this second fissure is costing. My friends at Pickering will be ever-so-happy to cover those expenses," Simone snapped.

Dom asked grimly, "Shall I tell the folks at Pickering this?"

"Oh no! It will be a distinct pleasure to tell them myself." Simone replied. "One more thing: When do you think the crane will arrive?"

"It's five-thirty now," Dom calculated. "It'll be about eight o'clock by the time the crane's in place. We should be able to start putting the tunnel back together soon after that."

"Okay, thanks," Simone said and exhaled.

Turning to Andy, Simone said, "I'd like to assemble senior staff to discuss this at seven a.m. sharp in the Speaker's office. I'll call the Chief and Captain Dupre. Dom, why don't you get some sleep? I'll see you in the Speaker's office. It's crucial that senior staff are all on the same page."

She dialed the Speaker's cellphone, thinking he'd gone to his Bethesda home. It shocked her when he answered on the second ring. "Simone? Are you okay?" he asked anxiously.

"Are you in your office at five-thirty in the morning?" she asked incredulously, but rushed on without waiting for an answer. "Listen, we need to talk. There's been another huge setback. First, I need to speak with Pickering on behalf of the U.S. government. I'll be up soon."

∽

"This had better be good," Vaughn snapped, glaring at Simone.

Simone's eyes narrowed as she said, "How dare you come into my office with that attitude? When I left this evening I had the distinct understanding that someone from Pickering would be on-site throughout the night. Now I find that you left at eleven-thirty, after giving the wrong coordinates. Coordinates, I might add, that led to the second collapse of the tunnel. So, let's cut right to the chase, shall we? Pickering is financially responsible for what's happened this evening. Moreover, I plan to bar Pickering Architects from competing for Federal contracts for the next seven years. Finally, I hope you've paid your professional liability insurance because I plan to hold you personally accountable for what has happened tonight. If you don't believe me, look it up in the Federal Acquisition Regulations!"

Vaughn sneered. "You can't do that; you need Pickering too much. As for the coordinates, how do you know they were wrong? The truth is you've managed this entire crisis poorly. You're not fit to be the Architect of the Capitol and you know it! I should have been chosen to be Architect of the Capitol, not you!"

Simone was silent for a long moment, then she said, her voice trembling with anger, "Oh, you are so wrong. You've done nothing but throw roadblocks into the entire search-and-rescue process. You've tried to drag out the evaluation of the Capitol, you've not worked with the engineers, and frankly, you have been less than kind to my staff. It is not my competence which is on the line, Vaughn, it's yours! As of this moment, you and Pickering no longer have a contract to work on the Capitol. You'll be hearing from the Speaker of the House later this morning.

"At seven a.m. senior staff will be meeting to figure out how to complete the search-and-rescue. As for you being more qualified to be Architect of the Capitol, you wouldn't last five minutes. To serve in this position, you need to be able to work with others—something you're completely incapable of! Now get out of my office. I have a meeting with the Speaker, and he's none too pleased!"

15

By six-forty-five, Simone had verbally fired Vaughn Hanesworth, awakened Chief Bentsen and Captain Dupre, and mentally drafted her own letter of resignation. Perhaps Vaughn was right: she was ill-equipped for the position of Architect of the Capitol. Her task now was to face the Speaker. Reviewing her initial assessments, Simone took a long walk down Pennsylvania Avenue, considering her options. As she walked, she clutched a bag of freshly baked croissants as if they were some sort of peace offering. She dreaded talking to the Speaker: she'd very much hoped to impress him.

She entered the reception area of the Speaker's office and knocked softly. Surprised, John McIntyre looked up from his desk, then jumped to his feet. "Simone, come in. Tell me what happened!" He gestured to the chair nearest the desk.

Simone sat down and sighed wearily. "I worked on struts until about ten-thirty last night. Then I went back to my office for a few hours of sleep. At four-thirty Dom woke me up. An hour earlier, the fissure we'd hoped to fix completely ruptured. Andy Taylor—he's the lead engineer in the tunnel—feels we're back to square one. There's a consensus that Vaughn Hanesworth miscalculated the pitch. This in turn stressed the struts and added to the torque. Instead of staying all night, Vaughn left at eleven-thirty and went home. Now with this damage, we have to start over."

Her shoulders slumped and she covered her face with her hands. Through tears she said, "I'll tender my resignation later today. I am totally responsible for this mess. Vaughn Hanesworth is right about one thing: I'm not competent enough for this position."

John reached across his desk and cupped her hands in his own. "Stop that kind of talk this instant! You're not responsible for this! Under no circumstances will I accept your resignation. In a few minutes, you and I will meet with Earl Bentsen, Paul Dupre, and the rest to figure out our next move. We'll get through this," he said gently. "And you'll still be the Architect of the Capitol."

"I'm so embarrassed! Crying is simply unprofessional! I don't know what came over me." She dabbed at her eyes.

"Ms. Perez. It means you're human like the rest of us." He stroked her hand and said, "Go ahead and use my restroom if you'd like to freshen up before the others arrive."

"Thank you. Please, excuse me."

While Simone took a moment to compose herself, Earl Bentsen walked in. "So, John, how's life treating you these days? I've got eight grand-kids; how about you?"

The two old friends shook hands warmly. "I'm up to six," said John. "My youngest daughter just had a baby girl. She's so precious; looks just like her mother at that age! Earl, listen, before the others arrive, give me your candid assessment of this situation. Specifically, how are we going to rescue the guys in the mechanical room? Not to mention Addie Hutchison and the others in the café."

Earl paused, then said, "You heard about the fissure?"

John nodded, "Simone just told me."

Earl winced, then said, "Well, the rupture of the fissure is a colossal setback, but it may be a blessing in disguise. The Rockville Engineering guys are excellent at what they do, but they're too concerned about the stability of the tunnel. They suspended the rescue efforts until further notice, although they're still working to shore up the fissure. From where I'm sitting, that's a moot point now. Luckily, Rob Tate helped me find a way into the mechanical room."

John lifted an eyebrow and said, "That young man's a smart one!"

Earl nodded and continued, "As you probably know, we've found an old elevator shaft just under an accessible bathroom. This shaft drops within feet of the mechanical room, so I'm recommending we work on that, pronto. One of my EMTs, Paula Winthrop, has been able to get to the mechanical room and medicate those fellows. Their rescue today is my highest priority."

As the two men chatted, Simone joined them. Her eyes were red and puffy, but with some fresh lipstick and a smile, she hoped no one realized how vulnerable she felt.

"Good morning, Chief. Thanks for getting here early. Shall we go down to the tunnel so you can see the rupture of the fissure firsthand?"

"Already did that, Simone," said the Chief. "I got here at six-fifteen and I walked the tunnel with Andy. He'll be here any minute. Something about needing to phone home and say hello to three little fellas before they leave for school. I gather my buddy Vaughn won't be here today?" Earl asked with a chuckle.

"Decidedly not! I'll be working with Lillian Hawkins in the Speaker's Office later today on terminating Pickering Architects. I considered throwing in my own resignation as well, but the Speaker has talked me out of it. For now." She looked down.

Earl eyed her for a long moment, then said, "Simone, let me be honest with you. There's not a thing I would have done differently. Not one thing! You've provided leadership, given appropriate direction, and dealt with the press. In my business, there's a lot of temptation to play the 'What if?' game. What if I'd gotten to the scene five minutes earlier? What if I'd had another ambulance? What if I'd rescued the middle floor first? Good firefighters don't allow themselves to ask those questions because they can eat you alive. Please, Simone, this has nothing to do with your competence!"

She gave a wan smile and nodded. Just then, Andy Taylor arrived with Dom.

"G'morning, Andy!" John stepped forward, hand outstretched. "I'm Speaker of the House, John McIntyre. Please, help yourselves to hot coffee and croissants. You're going to need them!"

They gathered around the conference table in the Speaker's office. John set the tone.

"Before we begin, let me thank each of you for all of the hard work you've done over the last forty-eight hours. You and your families are the real heroes in this tragedy. In a moment, we're going to set forth a plan to rescue the victims of the explosion. I'm here to listen and learn. However, I want to express my gratitude to each of you and those who serve under you. Often, the Congress seems like a bunch of people long on talk, but short on results. Nevertheless, I assure you there are members of Congress who are in awe of the work you're doing. If there's anything I can do to move the rescue process along, do not hesitate to ask."

Simone spoke up. "Thank you Mr. Speaker. We all know that the fissure has ruptured because of professional negligence by Vaughn Hanesworth. By the end of the day, Pickering Architects will no longer have a contract to work on the Capitol. Now we must decide how to rescue those trapped in the mechanical room and the café. I'm open to any and all ideas."

Andy spoke up first. "I walked the tunnel with Chief Bentsen about an hour ago," he said, leaning forward. "Frankly, the destruction is beyond belief. But the Chief is convinced this may not be all bad because it'll force us to think out of the box."

Turning to the Chief, he said, "I just spoke to my old supervisor who served three deployments to Afghanistan. He explained there's a new product on the market which allows medics to rescue patients in small places, like caves and such. In Iraq and Afghanistan this new system helped with a number of successful rescues. It works like this," Andy continued. "An airbag deploys. The device then burrows through the rubble. Once it has deployed ten feet, the first segment of the emergency evacuation tunnel locks into place. It continues this process, ten feet at a time. It may take some time, but we should be able to get the occupants out to safety."

"I saw this at a trade show recently," Earl volunteered. "It will work, I'm virtually certain. I can't believe I didn't think of it sooner! The only drawback is the emergency 'tunnel' only expands about two feet across. Most of the people in the café should be able to traverse the distance on their hands and knees. But Addie shouldn't be crawling. Besides the fact she has a broken shoulder, Addie's diabetes is unstable, making her too weak to traverse the tunnel. Let's take her out on a stretcher."

Andy spoke again. "Once the emergency evacuation tunnel is in place, I think Paula can easily get a stretcher down the emergency tunnel. Those stretchers are able to fold down to twelve inches. It will take two people, but that's not a problem. I can work with Paula on this so that when we actually get to the café, everyone will know what they're supposed to do in this phase. Earl, besides taking along Paula, I suggest you commandeer the services of one of those cadets; their brawn may come in handy."

"You're reading my mind, Andy. That's exactly what I'll do," Earl responded.

Simone cleared her throat. "All right, here's what we'll do. Chief, I want you to work with Rob on using the old elevator shaft to reach the basement floor and figure out exactly how far you are from the mechanical room and how we can get there safely. I'd like Paula to detail everything you'll need in order to evacuate the two gentlemen from the mechanical room to the Medevac helicopter.

"Andy, I want you to take the lead in making certain this new device will get us to the café. If everything goes well, we could get the café folks out later this evening. Let's come back in two hours and reassess. I want to make certain—and I mean absolutely certain—the tunnel can withstand the stress of this device. As much as we all want to rescue the café folks, this effort must not compromise our efforts to secure the tunnel. That said, this is outstanding work. Let's reconvene in two hours."

"Excellent!" Earl exclaimed. "I'll go check on the efforts to clear the elevator shaft. With any luck, we'll have a successful rescue on our hands."

The Speaker added, "I know this has been tough on everyone. I'm going to stay involved and help to see this through. If anything arises that you think I can help with, directly or otherwise, do not hesitate to call or come by. Thank you all!"

"Thanks, everyone!" Simone called out as they stood to leave.

◦◦

Lillian Hawkins rushed into the Speaker's Office uncharacteristically late. She'd overslept, something that never happened. To make matters worse, the Amtrak train from Baltimore to Washington arrived one hour behind schedule. When she finally reached her desk, the Speaker was waiting.

"Lillian. Grab some coffee and come on in. You and I have a lot to go over—and I'm short on time," John said, a hint of exasperation in his voice.

"Mr. Speaker, I am so sorry I am late! This is inexcusable!" Lillian said.

"Trust me, Lillian, you have absolutely nothing to worry about. Let me sum up what is going on and what I need you to do. Most of the tunnel completely collapsed last night. It's pretty clear it was negligence on the part of Vaughn Hanesworth and Pickering Architects. Simone Perez has verbally relieved him of his duties. However, we must fire him by the book. Please keep Simone and I apprised of your progress throughout the day. Begin by contacting John Sterling in the Office of General Counsel. He's expecting your call. Also, I spoke to Bob Harrington over in the Office of Government Ethics and he agreed to look over the termination document," John finished. He glanced at Lillian.

"I understand most of this," she said, putting down her coffee. "May I ask what will happen next with the rescue? I tossed and turned all night thinking of those guys in the mechanical room!"

John rubbed his eyes. "Chief Bentsen and Rob Tate found an old elevator shaft, not far from the mechanical room. We've hatched a plan, but it's going to be a crazy day around here, Lillian. Have I given you sufficient information to fire Hanesworth? What am I forgetting?"

Lillian nodded, "Mr. Speaker, I understand what needs to be done with the Hanesworth matter. Turning to your schedule," she pressed as John rolled his eyes, "you have a budget hearing this morning at ten, a call with the White House Chief of Staff about the Civil Rights Commission appointees at five-thirty, and—if I'm not mistaken—dinner with the Minority Whip, Harry Jones. I'll check to make sure I've not missed anything."

"Lillian, call Harry Jones and beg off," John pleaded. "He can be insistent, but just tell him I'll call once this crisis is over. I'm going to put in an appearance at the Budget hearing but I don't plan to stay."

Lillian excused herself and returned momentarily saying, "Mr. Speaker, I checked your calendar because I knew something was amiss. There are two things we overlooked. First, the House Education and Labor Committee is holding a markup of the Higher Education Amendments. You are supposed to drop by. Here are some remarks the staff put together. Finally, it's your grandson Jeremy's seventeenth birthday. Maybe call this evening, or text?" she said inquiringly.

John paused for a moment, then responded, "I'd completely forgotten about the Higher Education Amendments mark-up! That bill is in a bit of trouble, so I'll stop by briefly. And I'll call Jeremy this evening. Thanks, Lillian—I'm certain these two events would have gone unnoticed if you hadn't brought them to my attention!"

"Mr. Speaker, I'll absolutely keep Simone informed of our progress. I'll take good care of her, too." Lillian winked, then added sternly, "You'd best be off. I'll have all of the documents ready for your perusal by three this afternoon."

With that, Lillian Hawkins began the complex task of officially firing Vaughn Hanesworth and Pickering Architects.

As they lowered Rob Tate down the elevator shaft, utter darkness engulfed him. He flipped the light switch on his hard hat, but that provided only limited illumination. As he slowly descended one hundred feet Rob prayed *Please, Lord, help this to work.*

Down he went, further into what seemed like an endless abyss. Then his feet hit solid ground. It took a few moments for him to acclimate to this new environment. Dom turned on the floodlights, and at once Rob could see.

He turned ninety degrees, and what he saw amazed him. There, in the exact direction of the mechanical room was a long, narrow closet which ended two feet away from the elevator shaft. In a flash Rob realized the medics could probably hoist Billy and Fred through this closet and up the elevator shaft to safety!

Before he radioed the Chief and Dom he yelled, "Billy! Fred! Can you hear me?" He held his breath.

Then he heard, "Where are you, brother? It's time to go home!"

Rob couldn't hold back the tears. He cried for his buddies. He cried for himself, that he couldn't have prevented this horrible event from happening. He cried because he desperately needed sleep. Finally, Rob called out, "I'm going to get the rescue team! I'll be back real soon. Fellas, please tidy up."

With a hoarse voice he radioed the Chief, "Let's go. We've hit pay dirt!

Joel sat at his desk for the first time in three days, sorting through piles of paper and throwing stuff away. *Ah, but my secretary will be so pleased.*

He glanced over at Tyrone, diligently studying for a history exam on Friday.

"Is this test really important?" asked Joel.

Tyrone looked up from a thick text book with a serious look on his face. "Mr. Joel, you want me to come and work for you, right?" Joel nodded. "The only way my Gran will even consider your idea is if I can show her a good report card this quarter. With the part-time job I have, my studies have suffered some. Only way to get Gran's approval is to ace this midterm."

"I see your point. Can I help you study?" Joel really wanted this kid to succeed.

Tyrone shook his head. "Not right now. Maybe in a couple hours you can quiz me. Now I'm just going chapter by chapter, reviewing my notes. But at the end of the book they have these questions and I figure if I can get most of them right, I'm in good shape."

For about forty-five minutes, they sat in silence. Someone looking in on this scene might have assumed that these were two old friends, comfortably sharing tight quarters. Joel's cellphone disrupted the silence, its shrill ring causing both of them to jump.

"Joel, this is Charlie. Look I have it from a couple of folks that there's some sort of rescue effort taking shape. My source—who I've known for a long time and who I'll keep anonymous for now—is telling me they're very close to rescuing folks. Keep your ears open"

Before Joel could respond to Charlie, he received a text which simply said, "URGENT PRESS BRIEFING IN 45 MINUTES. PLEASE BE PROMPT. SIMONE PEREZ."

"There's a press briefing within the hour. I'll be in touch after that. How late will you be working?"

"I'm around for a while. Text me with regular updates!"

"Got it."

With that, study hall for Tyrone and Joel came to an abrupt end.

Makayla sat in the parking lot of the Sojourner Truth Elementary School in Washington D.C. She'd arrived at the school fifteen minutes early. *This should have been a day off*, she thought. She'd planned to take care of her chores in the morning and go shopping with one of her girlfriends in the afternoon. Now, she was going to take Jamal and James home, see that they got their homework done, and make sure they got a good night's sleep.

Then her cellphone rang.

"Makayla, this is Captain Dupre. Listen to me carefully. I know you've been working really hard this week, and you've got Addie's boys with you. This is what I'm hearing: they've got a new plan to rescue those trapped in the tunnel. They hope to get to the mechanical room in the next few hours. They're using some sort of new device to clear the way and there's a very real chance they could reach the café tonight. I can't order you in. I definitely wouldn't tell Addie's grandkids anything about this. My sense is that everything's going to happen at once. You're among my top officers I trust when stuff gets crazy. Please, I need you tonight."

Makayla swallowed a deep sigh and said brightly, "School gets out in ten minutes. Let me go home, feed and bathe the boys, and I should be there by five. I'll text Tyrone—maybe he can watch the boys."

"Makayla, you're the best. See you soon."

She sent a text to Tyrone explaining she planned to bathe the boys, feed them homemade beef stew, and then take them with her to work. She was surprised when he responded immediately. "SURE—I'M ON THE HILL NOW W/MR. JOEL. I CAN WATCH THEM. JUST LET ME KNOW WHEN YOU'RE HERE." Seconds later, he sent another text: "BEEF STEW? ANY EXTRA? <GRIN>"

16

SIMONE STEPPED UP TO the microphone.

"If everyone could please take your seat, we have a good deal to cover. The Speaker of the House, Congressman John McIntyre, will open with a few words. Mr. Speaker."

"Thank you, Ms. Perez." John took a deep breath, aware that his presence added to the gravity of the occasion. He gave a weary smile and began, "I have served in the U.S. Congress for over twenty-eight years—and ten of those years have been as Speaker of the House. I must tell you these have been, by far, the two most difficult days of my tenure here. I've also been proud because everyone, from the Congressional staff to the rescue crews and the maintenance staff, have been here throughout, helping to solve some very difficult problems. The press has covered this horrific event with talent, fairness, and grace, and for that I am truly grateful.

"In a moment, Ms. Perez will describe the rescue plan which has just been put into place. I think it is a bold strategy, and one which will work. It will require that everyone respects the other's role in this rescue effort. Therefore, I'm asking you—no, actually, I'm begging you—to respect the privacy of the victims during this rescue operation. I'm confident you will all rise to the occasion.

"One last thing—I want to publicly thank some people who've given unselfishly of their time and talents throughout this crisis. The first two individuals are Dom Martinelli, Director of Maintenance, and his assistant, Rob Tate. Neither of these two fellas has been home since early Monday morning and they've worked tirelessly to find solutions to some extremely difficult problems. Likewise, Captain Paul Dupre, with the Capitol Police, and Chief Earl Bentsen, with D.C. Fire and Rescue, have made outstanding contributions to this rescue effort.

"Finally, I would like to thank Simone Perez, Architect of the Capitol, who has kept each of you informed, worked through the tough architectural issues, and kept the various factions talking to each other. This extraordinary woman did this on almost no sleep. So, thank you, Simone, for your outstanding leadership! Let me turn this press briefing over to you."

As she took the podium, their eyes met and he winked. She chuckled and whispered, "Thanks, and I'm holding you to dinner, Mr. Speaker."

Turning to her notes, Simone said, "On behalf of everyone who has been working on the rescue efforts since the explosion occurred, I thank you, Mr. Speaker. Let me explain what has transpired since our last update and then I'll tell you how the rescue effort will proceed. As everyone knows by now, a major breech of the fissure occurred during the night. This has left the tunnel totally impassible. A group of senior staff met at seven o'clock this morning and we outlined a new rescue plan. It is a two-step process. First, we will rescue the two men in the mechanical room and get them the medical attention they urgently need. Then, a second team will attempt to rescue the occupants of the café. Let me fill you in on the details.

"With regard to gaining access to the mechanical room, we have discovered an old elevator shaft which is no longer used. As you can see with the visual we have up on the screen, this particular shaft drops within twelve feet of the mechanical room. Moreover, Rob Tate—who's become an expert on climbing through dusty, dirty old spaces within the U.S. Capitol—found there is a small closet which links directly over the mechanical room. Therefore, here is how we plan to proceed.

"Three medics from D.C. Fire and Rescue, headed by EMT Paula Winthrop, will first go into the mechanical room and rescue these two brave souls. Mr. Tate will assist Ms. Winthrop. Because these two men require immediate medical attention, there will be two medevac helicopters on the west lawn of the Capitol, waiting to transport them to Washington Hospital Center. There, a team of surgeons is standing by to attend to the major injuries to the leg of one of them. This is where we must ask you to restrain your coverage so that we can get these two fellows to the hospital as quickly as possible. Their families are leaving for the hospital now. The rescue effort is set to begin in fifteen minutes and—if all goes well—this phase of the rescue plan should be completed quickly.

"Once the first part of this plan has been executed, we will then turn to rescuing the occupants of the café. After we'd devised a plan for rescuing the guys in the mechanical room, we considered how we could reach the café. Through the discussions of our team, we realized we could utilize technology developed for military use in combat situations. This technology will burrow a temporary tunnel in increments of ten feet. Although the space is only two feet by two feet, we have verified that this product is suitable for the rescue of those trapped in the café. I'm particularly grateful to Andy Taylor with Rockville Engineering Associates for his leadership in helping us obtain this technology. At this moment, Andy is working with the Maintenance Department to deploy this device so that the second phase of this rescue mission will go smoothly."

Simone looked out over the press corps, each of them focused intently on her.

"Chief Earl Bentsen will head up the second phase of this rescue effort accompanied by Paula Winthrop, and Cadet Darrel Montgomery. Lieutenant Makayla Wainwright with the Capitol Police will also assist with this effort. We are not certain exactly how long it will take to get to the café using this new technology and the café rescue may very well take place in the wee hours of the morning. In any case, once we have cleared the café, we will be dispersing the victims a little differently. Since the majority of the occupants require little or no medical attention, an escort will take them to 2330 Rayburn Building where their loved ones await their release. There will be a physician present to attend to any medical needs they may have.

"Here's where I really need your help. I am sure that you as journalists are under pressure from your respective media outlets to 'get the story.' Nevertheless, I am asking you to refrain from approaching any of the victims until they reunite with their families.

"Before I open this up to questions, let me echo the Speaker's gracious remarks. There have been countless staff—most especially in my office— who've been working around the clock to help with a million and one odd tasks which have enabled us to formulate this rescue plan. If I mentioned them by name we'd be taking up valuable time. Just please know this: all of their contributions have been selfless and we owe them a debt of gratitude that can never be repaid."

Simone's voice cracked with emotion. She stood there for a moment, composing herself, and then asked, "Are there any questions?"

"Hi, Dave Phillips with the *New York Times*. Given the fact that Pickering Architects—and in particular Vaughn Hanesworth—have unique expertise in the historic preservation of the Capitol, why were they not involved in this final effort?"

Before Simone spoke, the Speaker stood up and gently took her elbow while whispering, "Let me handle this one."

"Hi, Dave. Glad you asked the question. Pickering Architects has indeed worked amicably with us on a variety of complex issues surrounding an edifice such as the Capitol. Regrettably, this fine working relationship fell apart, quite literally, last night. Without besmirching anyone's good name, or getting into who-did-what-to-whom, let me just advise you that this entire matter is in the hands of the General Services Administration. Since there's a possibility that this matter will end up in litigation, that's really all we can say on the matter. I'd advise all of you to contact GSA if you need additional information."

Joel Carlson stood and said, "Ms. Perez, I just want to clarify what will be happening to the café occupants. If I understand you correctly, members of the press should wait to interview anyone until each person meets their loved ones. But will there be any opportunity to interview them after they've been attended to by a physician?"

Simone moved to the microphone. "Joel, I think that's going to be up to each individual. I'd imagine there may be time to chat briefly, although I'd hope any interview would be very brief as these folks are probably exhausted and hungry.

"That's it, folks. Thanks for your patience throughout this crisis!" Simone said.

～

Earl gazed at a clipboard one last time to make certain everything was in order. He looked at Paula and Rob and said, "Okay, let's review this one more time. Once you reach the mechanical room, Paula's going to livestream a video from her phone to mine. I will be right there with you the whole time. Rob, you must cut the steam pipe carefully, then lift it so Paula can free Billy's leg. Do either of you have any questions so far?"

Rob sighed and said, "No, sir." Then, hesitating, he added, "It's just . . . I'm afraid I could hurt Billy when I cut the pipe. He's already in so much pain."

Before Chief Bentsen could answer, Paula spoke up forcefully, "Rob, I understand how you feel. However, you're not in this alone. I'll be right there with you, guiding you so you cut the pipe cleanly and away from my patient. Plus, Earl will be right there too, watching us carefully."

"Paula's right! The three of us will get through this together. Now listen, don't be afraid to ask me questions. This is a tough rescue situation and we need to lean on one another. Understood?" Rob and Paula nodded simultaneously.

Earl continued, "Once you free Billy's leg, Paula will bandage him and prepare him for transport. Paula, do you have the Demerol we discussed earlier?"

Paula nodded affirmatively.

"Okay, good. Once he's ready for transport, I want the two of you to work together to get him into the harness; take your time. It's more important that we get Billy out safely. If it takes some extra time, so be it! Once his harness is on, the two of you will have to lift him and carry him to the little closet space. Once he's in the closet, you'll need to attach the harness to safety straps which are already in the closet. After you secure the safety straps, the two medics who will be waiting just outside the closet will take over and pull Billy and Fred up the elevator shaft to safety. Any questions?" Earl looked at both of them intently.

"Nope. Let's go, Paula, and get this thing done," Rob said.

Paula eagerly agreed and began climbing the ladder, lugging her gear. As planned, she went into the crawlspace first. Rob followed close behind her, dragging some extra tools they might need in order to extract Fred and Billy.

Just before they entered the mechanical room, Paula said, "Look, no matter what, stay positive when we're in the mechanical room. Don't kid yourself: Billy may not comprehend the words we're saying, but he'll surely get the gist of what we say. So keep it positive."

They made it to the mechanical room and Paula sang out, "Okay, boys, party's over. Time to get you two fruitcakes out of here. You've been loitering on Federal property for far too long."

As Paula began to attend to her patients, two things alarmed her. First, Billy's fever was back because he looked flushed. It bothered her even more that Fred did not respond. She yelled, "Hey, Fred, ready to go home?"

He opened his eyes and nodded. They needed to get these guys to the hospital immediately.

They got to work right away, attending to Billy's needs first. Paula put Earl Bentsen on speakerphone.

"Rob, I'm staying right here with you; we'll do this thing together, okay? Now, see if you can cut through the boiler pipe. Go slow. Your goal is to simply free his leg. Try to stay as far away from his leg as possible."

Rob swallowed hard and said a silent prayer for guidance. He had to get this right!

Rob found a part of the pipe, just to the right of Billy's knee, which seemed like the best extraction point. Slowly, carefully, Rob began to saw the pipe, mindful not to touch Billy. It seemed to take forever. Rob felt droplets of sweat fall from his brow as he rhythmically sawed back and forth. Suddenly, without any warning, the saw stopped! Rob put all of his strength into it, but the saw would not budge.

"Hang on a second, Chief. We've got a problem. Let me see something." Rob looked at the pipe from a different angle and grimaced. "Well, Chief, the saw blade is bent beyond repair. I brought a spare but I need to get the old blade out. That baby's stuck in there. Let me take the saw handle off, and see what we have."

Earl Bentsen thought for a moment, then said, "Rob, do you have any sort of lubricant with you? Maybe something you'd use to repair an old hinge or something? My daddy always said grease of any kind could get a fella out of a world of trouble."

Rob thought for a minute, then said, "I've got a tiny bit of graphite in my bag. Let me go get it, plus a new blade. Let's see if I can do this. Hang on a second."

Swiftly he retrieved the new blade and graphite. He put the new blade in the saw and said a silent prayer that this would work. Carefully he drizzled the graphite along the sides of the stuck blade. He tried to remove the old blade again, but it didn't budge. Then Rob lay on the floor and reached up, grabbing the blade with both hands. Again, nothing happened. Finally he said, "Paula, hand me the long-nosed plyers. They're in the little pocket on the side of my bag."

"Sure, hang on." Paula stood up and retrieved the plyers. As she did, Billy began to wake up, emitting a low moan. Paula turned and, in a soothing voice, said "It's going to be all right. In just a few more minutes, you'll be out of here. Close your eyes and rest."

Briefly, Billy half opened his eyes and for a moment, tried to speak. Just as quickly, he closed his eyes again, falling back into an uneasy slumber.

Paula handed Rob the plyers and he began to move the bent blade back and forth, like a stubborn old weed. At first, his progress was imperceptible. Finally, the damaged blade came loose. Without stopping, he began sawing the pipe again, this time with slow, deliberate strokes. All at once, the pipe split in two. Rob grabbed the pipe firmly with both hands and hoisted it high, far away from Billy's leg, panting with exhaustion.

"I think we're there, Chief. I'm going to stop streaming this so I can properly bandage Billy for transport," said Paula.

"Nice work, both of you!" Earl exclaimed. "I'll see you up here in a few minutes. Let's get these guys to the hospital."

Paula began to attend to Billy's needs. As she did, she was aware of Rob standing opposite her, helping her as she bandaged the limb. It took forty-five minutes to get Billy ready to go and secure the harness around him. Then, they carefully hoisted their unconscious patient up through the long closet, taking great care to make certain not to bump his injured leg. Once they were through the closet, two other medics took over. It took only minutes to get Billy up the ancient elevator shaft where a Medevac team took over. Immediately they started a blood transfusion, hooked him up to monitors, and rushed him to the waiting helicopter.

Within minutes, Paula received verification via radio that Billy was in route to Washington Hospital Center. The team of experts accompanying him to the hospital was fairly certain Billy would pull through!

She heaved a sigh of relief as she turned to Fred. His blood pressure had dropped dramatically, with slow labored breaths. Paula shouted, "Rob, quick! Fred isn't doing too well. Throw me the harness."

Paula and Rob gently sat Fred up. Blood spewed from his shoulder area.

"This is much worse than I thought," Paula said. "Let's go!"

As they lifted Fred up into the small closet, Paula wadded some gauze, pressing it into the wound. Soon, the two medics near the elevator shaft took over, helping Fred to safety. All Paula could say was, "Medevac team, Fred is extremely critical. Recommend emergency chest X-ray en route."

Addie Hutchison felt edgy and irritable, though she didn't know why. It thrilled her that the two men in the mechanical room would soon be in the hospital, getting the care they needed.

Still, Addie could not shake her apprehension as she sat quietly in the café, lost in her own thoughts.

What's going to happen next?

Her health didn't worry her, although she knew they would have to fix her shoulder. Addie worried about her boys. How could she possibly care for them with her arm in a sling? When would she be able to return to work? She had to keep a steady income in order to keep her little family going. While she had some sick leave, she hated to waste it on her own health needs. She'd tried to save that leave in case one of the boys needed her. All of these questions kept running through her mind—even after she'd tried to calm down.

Her single most important question concerned her beloved Tyrone. Addie knew for sure he had been up to something lately. He'd been cranky in the mornings and he wouldn't look her in the eye. Because Tyrone was her first grandchild, they had always had a special relationship. When he was little, they would play hide-and-seek. Addie could still hear his giggles when she would find him in a cupboard or curled up under the stairwell. Those were precious days. Now they were playing a different game of hide-and-seek. In this particular game, Tyrone did not want to be found.

I'm going to have a very long talk with that young man when I get home.

Just then Barbara piped up, "Addie, you're entirely too quiet! Now either you need something else to eat, or something's on your mind. Which is it?"

"I declare, Barbara, you know me too well!" Addie laughed. "I'm fine. Okay, I'm worried about the boys. If they put me in a cast, how'm I gonna cook and clean? I need to work so I can provide them with a decent home. I'm sorry, but it's the uncertainty that has me worried."

Addie looked at Barbara through weary eyes. Although she had slept some, this ordeal had taken a toll on her.

"Addie, lots of things are different now. For one thing, you have some new friends and we're not going to let you down. I might be wrong, but my guess is the Senate Food Services folks will take care of you. Besides, look around you. They have a bit of fixing up to do here in the café."

Barbara tried to offer comforting words. Still, she had to admit Addie probably had a tough road ahead.

Jim felt for his cane and walked over to the table where Addie and Barbara were talking. "Addie," he said, "I've got the crazies too! I am worried about my wife, about work, about everything! It's driving me out of my mind. You are definitely not alone. But there's something that I'm absolutely sure of."

"What's that?" Addie asked.

"You and I are survivors! We've known what adversity is and we've known for a very long time. So we will pick ourselves up, get our bearings, and move on," Jim said. Then with a grin he added, "Of course, it may also be that you and I have both gone 'round the bend. No worries. I'll make sure they assign us to the same rubber room. Just think of the fun we'll have!"

Addie's laughter spilled over and when she finally gained control of herself she said, "Mr. Jim, you are one funny dude!"

❧

The occupants of the café were thrilled to hear they would soon be out and on their way home. Even Bruce smiled. Barbara wanted to help in the rescue but Paula dissuaded her. Dan Larson sat at a table, his Bible opened to a portion of Psalm 118 which read:

"Hark, glad songs of victory in the tents of the righteous:

The right hand of the Lord does valiantly . . .

I shall not die, but I shall live,

and recount the deeds of the Lord."

He said a silent prayer from his heart, full of pleading, yet also enormous hope. He felt this hope as a young priest on Easter morning. He prayed, "Oh Lord, thank you for bringing us to this place. I ask that you'll follow each person as they leave this café. I will never forget them. Thank you, Lord, because through this whole rotten mess I'm renewed. Now give me the strength to go back into the world—a world which so desperately needs your hope. When I stumble again, remind me of your grace, which I live in day by day. Lord, please watch especially over Bruce. Let me never forget to sing a song of thanksgiving!"

17

CHIEF BENTSEN STUDIED THE workings of the Emergency Evacuation Tunnel one last time. He'd chosen his star cadet, Darrel Montgomery, to assist with the rescue because he had proven himself as a hard worker throughout this ordeal. Darrel knew very well that lives depended on their success.

"Darrel, do you have the pickaxe ready? Who knows what we'll need to clear out once we reach the café."

"Yes, sir. I strapped the tools we'd need to the gurney I'm hauling in. Who's going with us, sir? I ask because there are several dogleg turns that look rather tricky," Darrel said.

"We have Paula Winthrop, who you know. Officer Makayla Wainwright is with the Capitol Police Force. She knows her stuff. One of the café victims, Addie Hutchison, will need to ride on the gurney. I'll help you," Earl said.

As the two men discussed the mission amongst themselves, Paula walked up. "Gentlemen, I don't mind telling you it will be a relief to get this rescue behind us. This has been a terrible crisis for these folks, not to mention their families."

"Paula, how are the two guys who were rescued from the mechanical room. Will they make it?" Darrel asked.

"Yes, I think so, although one of the men has severe trauma to his leg. They are in good hands," Paula said.

Makayla walked up just then. "Hello y'all! I'm Makayla Wainwright with the Capitol Police. Captain Dupre asked me to escort you to and from the café. Are there any last-minute things I can help with?" she asked, smiling.

"No, Makayla, but I do have a couple questions. At the end of the temporary tunnel we're going through, there's a little dogleg turn. Can you guide us through it when we get there? Additionally, we'll need an eight-foot turning radius for the gurney. Can we do that?" Earl asked.

Makayla thought for a minute, then said, "Chief Bentsen, we'll be able to do it. We may need to turn the gurney around in the entrance to the café. Look, we are essentially going to be walking through a very long tent, right?"

Earl nodded, so Makayla continued.

"At the end of that tent, there should be just enough space to maneuver the gurney, just outside the temporary tunnel. We should be fine, Chief Bentsen."

"Please, I'm Earl, and this is Darrel. Thanks for coming with us."

As Earl spoke, Andy and Dom walked up.

"Are you all ready to start? It looks like everything is in order. Do you have any last-minute questions for any of us?" Andy asked.

Earl thought for a moment, then said, "I'll take the lead, and I'd like Makayla to come directly behind me since she knows this tunnel best. Then, Darrel, please help Paula with the gurney. We're planning to carry tools as well as medical supplies on the gurney.

"Let's do this, folks," Earl said as he climbed into the Emergency Evacuation Tunnel.

At first, the team found it to be slow going. Earl and Makayla couldn't go very fast crawling on all fours. Fortunately, Maintenance had some lighting rigged up, so it wasn't too difficult to find their way. Soon they were making progress and Earl made certain he radioed Andy at regular intervals.

Darrel and Paula found the trip very difficult. As they dragged the gurney with the equipment, it became a push-and-pull proposition. Several times they had to back up several feet in order to center the gurney and its load. Paula called out, "Yo, Earl. Can you please tell us about these turns ahead of time? This gurney doesn't have power steering!"

Before Earl could answer, Makayla said, "Sorry, Paula. We're going through a short turn which is about thirty degrees to your left. If you take it slow, you'll be fine."

Something about Makayla's comments made Paula chuckle. They progressed at a snail's pace. After what seemed to be hours, the rescue team arrived at the dogleg. Earl and Makayla climbed through without any difficulty. Soon they were standing at the entrance to the café. "Makayla, you wait here a minute. I don't want to sound macho or anything, but that gurney's going to require two men to get through that turn."

"Yes, I agree," Makayla answered.

Soon all four of them stood before the entrance to the café. Darrel began to swing the pickaxe, deftly finding the frame of the doorway. Finally, the debris gave way and Darrel opened the entrance door.

The café occupants heard the sound of a pickaxe chipping away at the rubble. Earl Bentsen and Darrel Montgomery worked slowly, making sure to clear out what was left of the doorway. Tension in the café grew as the rescuers moved rubble and dirt in order to have a safe passageway for their charges. Finally, Earl and Paula were at the doorway and they waited a moment until Darrel got the auxiliary light on. All at once, light transformed the dark, musty café. The café occupants had to squint to see.

Finally, Chief Bentsen asked in a booming voice, "Anybody in here want to go home? I am D.C. Fire Chief Earl Bentsen and I am in charge of your rescue. Please, stay where you are for a few more moments and do exactly what I ask you to; it'll make my job easier and we can get you all out quicker. EMT Paula Winthrop and I are trained medics. We need to look carefully at each of you. Then, we'll help you make your way through the Emergency Evacuation Tunnel. Once you're outside we will take you to the Rayburn Building, where your loved ones are waiting. I must ask each of you to cooperate with this procedure. Do not—and I repeat do not—leave the premises of the Capitol grounds until you have been cleared to do so by medical staff. The U.S. Government is responsible for rescuing you and making sure each of you receives any medical attention you may need as a result of the explosion."

Earl Bentsen then turned to Paula. "Let's look at Ms. Hutchison first, then triage the rest."

Just then Makayla peeked in and said, "Hey girl! I am mighty glad to see you." She walked over and hugged Addie for several minutes, tears streaming down both of their faces.

"Makayla, did you go by the house? Are my boys okay?"

"Addie, I got your boys. They've been with me most of the time—driving me nuts, too! Matter of fact, they're waiting for you if Chief Bentsen says you're up to it"

"So you're Addie Hutchison?" Earl Bentsen asked.

"I'm right here and I want to go home," Addie was crying.

"I bet you do. Let me see this shoulder, Miss Addie, while Paula checks your blood sugar." Earl gently moved Addie's shoulder and she cried out in pain. "Darrel, I need the sling, pronto. Please bring some gauze to cushion the clavicle, too." Within seconds Darrel returned and helped Earl temporarily set the shoulder. Then Earl turned to Paula as they looked at her blood sugar results. "Well, Miss Addie, these numbers aren't too bad, given what you've gone through. Paula, let's give her 100 milligrams of Demerol to keep her comfortable. Addie, we're going to put you on this gurney and push you through the emergency tunnel we just came through. The others will crawl, but you're getting the royal treatment!"

Barbara allowed Paula to look her over, but she was fine. Paula then turned to Jim. As she took his vital signs and listened to his chest, Jim quipped, "I can't see a thing!"

"Well, Mr. Stenson, I can't fix that," laughed Paula, "But word has it you've got the best ears in the joint. You're good to go! It's my understanding your wife has been in close contact with Congressman Chamberlin's office since they've been informing families of the situation. Anyway, your wife sends her love, and asked us to tell you she's anxiously awaiting your arrival at home."

"That's my gal, always sensible! Thanks, Paula, for everything!" Jim said as he gave Paula a huge hug.

Barbara walked toward the emergency tunnel, Jim Stenson by her side, the two of them laughing as they helped each other.

Finally, Earl Bentsen looked at Father Dan. "Well, Father, I know your wife and daughter are eager to see you. Look at my finger and follow it. Let me take this flashlight and look into your eyes. Hmmm. It looks like you've had a concussion and they'll want you to go to the hospital—but let's go find your family first."

Finally, Earl walked over to Bruce Graham. "You must be Bruce Graham. Let me see that hand. I can tell you right now that hand is badly broken. Darrel, get the large splint and ace bandage. This will at least stabilize it until you see your family and then we'll get you to the hospital. I want you to take this pain killer."

"I'll be fine. I have no family. I'm planning to go to a 'Doc-in-the-box' and go home. I need sleep," said Bruce.

"Young man, my list has someone in the Rayburn Building waiting for you. Therefore, that's where I am taking you. I strongly urge you not to go to some walk-in place. I can tell you your hand needs the attention of an expert, not some first-year medical student. I am pretty sure you need surgery." Earl Bentsen recognized that he needed to be firm with Bruce.

Once Earl completed his medical assessment of the café occupants, he quickly huddled with Darrel. Soon, everyone inched into the emergency tunnel. Barbara and Jim led the pack, with Bruce trying to crawl yet protect his hand. Behind him, Father Dan made his way as Makayla helped guide him. Earl and Darrel guided the gurney, carefully doing their best to avoid bumps. They hadn't gone far when Father Dan cried out, "Wait! Could one of you fellas please go back in and grab my Bible? It's on the second table."

"Sure, Father," Darrel said as he quickly retrieved Dan's Bible from the café. Soon the weary caravan found its way through the rubble-filled tunnel and out of the building. The swiftness of their rescue took Father Dan by complete surprise. Although they knew the imminence of their rescue, it still came as a shock. Dan found it difficult to comprehend what was happening. When they cleared the temporary tunnel, a Humvee awaited them. Earl helped them into the huge vehicle, one by one. As the roadway became smoother, Earl Bentsen started to chuckle.

Then Father Dan heard a sound he would remember for the rest of his life; as the Humvee emerged from the tunnel a large crowd cheered and clapped. Some people cried.

Dan saw a heavyset man speak into a walkie-talkie: "Simone, they are all free now, and headed for the Rayburn Building. Thank heaven this crisis is finally over."

18

A LOUD CHEER WENT up in room 2330 of the Rayburn Building where anxious family members had been waiting for almost three days. They hugged one another and several people cried softly. Now, they could finally go home and put the ordeal of the past three days behind them.

Colleen Larson felt bewildered by the news that Dan had reached safety. The combination of her fatigue and raw emotion made her feel as if she were living out her life in slow motion. The victims were safe! She should be celebrating! Yet, Colleen sat silently holding her daughter's hand. Although she felt grateful for her husband's freedom, Colleen only had two thoughts: *When can I see Dan, and how soon can we go home?*

Amy sat patiently by her mother's side, seeking to comfort her. A part of Amy wanted to tell her mom to snap out of it.

Daddy is on his way here right now!

She recognized she could never fully understand the depth of her mother's emotions.

I suppose twenty-eight years of marriage will do that to a person.

Noise interrupted Amy's private thoughts. Then someone cried out, "Get ready; here they come!"

Amy saw his clerical collar first as tears came to her eyes. "Mom, there's Daddy!" Colleen stood now, crying as Amy called out, "Daddy, Daddy! Over here—we're over here!"

At first, Father Dan heard his daughter's voice but he could not see her. Dan's eyes refused to focus. Then he saw them and the crowd made way for him. Finally, he stood before Colleen who rose to meet him. He put his arms around her. Husband and wife held one another for a long time; Colleen cried softly and Dan held her close, grateful to finally have her in his arms. After a while, the couple's embrace broadened to include their beloved daughter. Colleen finally broke the silence; "Honey, I'm not letting you out of my sight for a very long time!"

∾

Joel sat next to Tyrone, who tried hard to keep the twins quiet.

"You two little bros settle down this instant!" Tyrone said firmly. "If you two don't stop acting like clowns, you're not going to see Gran. They're gonna say you two little boys are just too noisy."

James and Jamal sat down, trying hard to be good. Joel offered both boys a stick of gum in hopes that would satisfy them for a bit.

Joel was a wreck. He felt torn in several directions. He knew Tyrone needed him, although the boy would never admit that. The reporter in Joel knew there were any number of human interest stories in this room. A dutiful reporter for *The Washington Post* would be working the crowd in the room. Joel longed to see Barbara safe!

Joel, so lost himself in thought, he did not hear Tyrone at first.

"Mr. Joel, come say hello to my Gran. See, she's right over there—the one in the wheelchair."

When Joel did finally looked up, he saw her calling out, "There they are! My boys are all right. Oh thank the Lord! Get over here!"

James and Jamal raced over to their grandmother and began chattering.

"Hi, Gran! Why do you have your arm in a sling? I got an A on my math test today. Not supposed to tell you, but Tyrone got a job at night. I love you, Gran!"

Tyrone strode over to Addie, with Joel following behind him. "Hey Gran!" he leaned down and held her, trying not to cry.

"What's this business about a job?" Addie asked.

"Well, Gran, here's the truth. I was worried about you. I saw you skipping your medicine sometimes, so I got a job. I left the house after you went to bed and worked at night stocking the shelves of a CVS. I earned six hundred dollars and I saved every penny for you. "

Addie cried and hugged her eldest grandson. "I knew you were up to something but I thought maybe you had a girlfriend. Honey, you don't need to work like that. We'll make it somehow. The Lord's gonna provide."

"Gran, I quit that job today. Listen, I think you know Mr. Joel. He's with *The Washington Post,* and he's helped me a lot the last three days. He's a good man."

"Hello, Addie! It's great to see you safely out of the cafe. You have three fine young men here and you ought to be very proud of them. When you're feeling better, I want to talk to you about Tyrone."

Addie's eyes narrowed. "Might as well tell me what he did now. No sense in waiting."

Joel laughed and said, "Oh, no Addie. He's a great kid. All I want to speak with you about is allowing him to do an internship with me for three months, maybe longer. He would come to my office after school each day and do research or run errands, that sort of thing. I think Tyrone has a bright future."

Addie smiled and said, "We can talk later. But it sounds like you're one who knows what he is doing."

Then, for some unexplained reason, Addie started to chuckle!

❧

Joel felt someone take his hand, but he assumed one of the twins wanted another piece of gum.

Then Joel looked down. Barbara smiled up at him and said, "Buy a girl dinner? I hear you fellas at *The Post* know how to treat a woman right!"

"Barbara!" Joel exclaimed as he put his arms around her as tears of joy filled his eyes. Finally, she was safe.

"Barbara, this has been the hardest three days of my life!"

At first, Barbara laughed, then tears came to her eyes as she said, "I want a hot shower, a cold Coke, and you. I've missed you so much. Without the internet, it was simply maddening. I knew you'd be worried sick. Can we just go home? I love you, Joel."

❧

Slowly, the room began to clear out as family members took their loved ones either home, or to the hospital. They cleared Bruce, but only after they'd scheduled an appointment with a hand surgeon for first thing in the morning.

Turning to leave, he saw her: Shelley stood before him and looked him in the eye.

"Hello, Bruce," she said. "I've been waiting for you. Please don't be angry with me. I tried your office several times Monday morning. Then, when I heard about the explosion, I was really concerned."

"Shelley, I'm not angry, not at all. Why do you even care? I mean we're divorced, well almost."

"Bruce, that's why I tried calling you. I hadn't slept in days. I just kept thinking that . . . that we should give our marriage another try." Shelley's eyes glistened with tears.

He stood there trying to understand Shelley's words. He couldn't get over the fact she was actually there. For him.

"Look, I'm having difficulty processing what you're saying. I'm absolutely stunned to find you here—to know you care. It's overwhelming, in a good way."

"Listen, maybe I should just go. Who am I kidding? You probably have someone else . . ." Shelley turned to leave.

"Shelley, no. Wait. There's no one else. You want the truth? The truth is while I was stuck in the café I had plenty of time to think. I thought about regrets, about the fact that my own brothers don't even speak to me anymore. But my biggest regret," he said as his voice cracked, "was losing you. Look, I'm tired and hungry and I need you. Please, let's go get some food, get this prescription filled, and go to my place. We'll take this very slow. Please, don't leave again."

"Are you certain?" she asked.

"Positive. I don't want you to go. We have work to do on our marriage. I think I want to try. This will be tough. I will try . . . really try. I do have a favor to ask. I'm having my hand operated on in the morning, and I'm scared. Please, go with me."

"I'd be glad to," Shelley replied. "Let's go."

19

JOHN MCINTYRE GLANCED AT the number on his phone. "Hello, Paul. It looks like we're out of the woods. Thanks for all you've done."

"Mr. Speaker, I called to let you know I've completely secured the tunnel to all traffic and I've sent home the officers who were here all night. I have a quick report to type and then I'll be off duty as well. I'll check in with you on Monday."

As John hung up the phone, Dom walked into the Speaker's office to tell Simone the good news, "Simone, all of the café survivors are now safely in the Rayburn Building! We're finally done. Survivors are now with their loved ones. We'll transport several of the survivors to Washington Hospital Center for medical attention. The engineer guys have gone home, and all of my team has left. Even Rob's gone home! I'm leaving as soon as I go by my office and shut off my computer. I think Chief Bentsen is coming down here."

"Oh Dom, I can't thank you enough for the leadership you've provided through this entire nightmare," Simone said.

Dom grinned and shrugged. "I was just doing my job. Besides, if I'd been more careful, maybe this whole thing could have been prevented." Dom's voice trailed off.

The Speaker looked intently at Dom and said, "Mr. Martinelli, if you think this is your fault, you are absolutely mistaken. This was an accident. It could have happened to anyone. I'd hate to think you are bearing responsibility for this. That would be wrong!"

"Well, I appreciate your kind words. However, I have supervisory responsibility here. We must not overlook that fact. Anyway, I'm going home. Simone, I'll be off tomorrow."

"Fine, Dom. Please get some rest!" Simone called to him as he walked away.

Simone turned back to the Speaker just as Chief Bentsen walked in. He looked exhausted but managed to smile. "Mr. Speaker, Ms. Perez, I'm delighted to inform you that we've completed our rescue mission. It took sixty-eight hours, but everyone will be all right. Now I'm supposed to tell you that, on behalf of the D.C. government, we look forward to working with you in the future. Honestly though, I don't! Maybe after a couple of nights' sleep I'll feel differently. But this one was a real doozy!"

"Well, Chief, you could surely improve the services provided by the D.C. government." John said with a bit of a twinkle in his eye.

"How's that, Mr. Speaker?" the Chief asked.

"You can run for mayor. I'll help you! If you get serious, I'll chair your campaign." John said.

"Mr. Speaker, I'm honored that you think so highly of me. It cheers my soul. Nevertheless, I'm a fire-and-rescue guy. That's it. Besides, my wife will leave me. I've been married forty-four years, I've got eight grandkids. Why on this earth would I run for mayor?"

"I think if you ever ran for mayor, you'd bring excellence to D.C. government. You know how people think and act. That's all politics is about: knowing how to read what people are really saying. As far as Leena leaving you, that's not going to happen, Earl. Think about it," John said grinning.

"I'm going home to Leena now. I'll tell her you send your regards. Simone, let's have coffee next week and figure out how D. C. Fire & Rescue can support your staff while they fix that fissure! Good night, or I guess its good morning."

Simone stood up stretched and said, "John, I think I'll head home too. I won't be in the office but I'll log on later today and see what further work I need to do to fire Vaughn."

John got up and stood before her, and held both of her hands in his own. Then he said softly, "Have dinner with me tonight. I'm asking you out because I want to pursue a relationship. You're bright and capable. Moreover, I have fun with you! Don't worry, I promise I will not hurt you!" Then, he gently kissed her.

His kiss surprised her and Simone stood silent for a moment. Then she smiled and said, "John, how about I fix an early dinner tonight? You can come over at six and we'll make it an early night since we are both sleep-deprived. Does that sound good?"

"That sounds about perfect," John said. "I do have one question: Will you play the cello for me?"

"That will be my pleasure, John."

With that, Simone Perez, Architect of the Capitol, picked up her things and went home.

∾

Rob arrived home at nine-forty-five in the morning. Anna was at work and the girls were at school. It seemed strange to be at home alone in the middle of the day. The grandfather clock in the living room ticked off the minutes, reminding him he'd missed too much time from home this week. He went to the kitchen, deciding to have breakfast before going to sleep. As he poured himself a bowl of cereal, he saw someone had obviously spilled some milk this morning. They had cleaned it up a bit hastily, leaving telltale puddles of milk on the kitchen floor. It had to be his youngest daughter, Hanna. She always ran late in the mornings. It drove her mother crazy, but Rob laughed it off.

Rob was glad to be home, yet he felt somehow sad. How he wished the girls were home; they always cheered him up. He thought of this awful week. Although the physical demands of the job had been tough, the emotional demands had been more than Rob could handle. He thought of Billy waking up from surgery without his left leg. Once again, Rob asked himself why he hadn't skipped the staff meeting. Perhaps things would have turned out differently. He took his dishes to the sink, cleaned up the remnants of this morning's mishaps, and headed to bed.

He rummaged through his drawers until he found an old flannel shirt and his old sweat pants. Anna continually threatened to throw his sweats out, claiming they had more holes than a slice of Swiss cheese. Somehow, the smell of his freshly laundered shirt gave him comfort. He noticed Anna had taken the time to make their bed and straighten their room. He turned down the bedspread and slipped in between the flannel sheets. It felt so good to lie down in his own bed. It felt so good to be home.

He was exhausted, yet sleep would not come. Rob closed his eyes, reliving the images of the week in his mind. He saw the long, dusty vent space stretching before him, the conversations with the café occupants in their desperation, the kind concern of Simone Perez for his safety, the quiet resolve of Chief Bentsen that no lives be lost on his watch, and the horror of removing the pipe from Billy's mangled leg.

As he lay there, he heard the front door open, then quietly shut. Before he could get up and investigate, the bedroom door opened. Without a word

Anna slipped beside Rob, wrapped her arms around him and whispered, "I love you, Rob. I always have and I always will."

There, in Anna's arms, Rob sobbed like a child for several minutes before falling into a deep restful sleep.

❧

Simone Perez sat by Addie Hutchison's bedside, dozing off. Doctors had operated on Addie's badly broken shoulder in the wee hours of the morning. Now, she slept quietly, an IV helping to keep her diabetes in check. Although Addie had a long recovery ahead, she would be fine.

Last night had been difficult for everyone involved. D.C. Fire and Rescue, as well as the engineers, worked tirelessly to successfully rescue the café customers. The Capitol tunnel remained closed indefinitely; there was at least three months of work ahead to fix the enormous fissure. Thankfully, no lives had been lost. Between helping the rescue team and discussing the next steps with the Speaker it had been a challenging night, to say the least.

Simone had arrived home at dawn, falling into bed. She'd slept for a few hours, then drove to the hospital to be with Addie, concerned she might need something. Now, as she dozed in her chair, she wondered how she could ever be ready for a date with John McIntyre this evening. Although cooking a romantic meal seemed like a good idea at five-thirty in the morning, it seemed like a daunting task now. Then it hit her: Padrones! She whipped out her cellphone and texted Anthony, the owner's son and explained her dilemma. He happily helped her. She ordered manicotti, with cannoli for dessert. When he texted, "What kind of wine?" She answered "Nonalcoholic." He had a light imported sparkling cider from Spain that would work nicely. Dinner would arrive at six o'clock sharp. Now, if she could sleep a bit, she'd be fine.

She dozed for an hour, but Addie's low moan awakened her.

"Where am I? Where are my boys?" Addie asked.

Simone took her hand and said, "Addie, you're in the hospital. The boys are at school. Everyone thought it would be best for you to rest."

Addie looked at her for a long moment then recognized Simone. "You came to help me! Thank you so much. Did they fix my arm?"

"They did, indeed! I didn't talk to the doctors, but I understand you'll be going home in a few days, as soon as your diabetes is under control. Makayla is bringing the boys over around six-thirty. Can I get you something?"

A nurse came in to give Addie a shot for the pain and something to drink. Addie sipped her drink, trying to overcome her grogginess. Her shoulder was in excruciating pain. "How am I ever gonna take care of my boys? Plus, I got to get back to work next week! I need my paycheck!"

"Addie, honey, you won't be going to work for several weeks. They have closed the café indefinitely. Since this happened while you were at work, you're eligible for Worker's Comp. You won't miss a paycheck, I promise." Simone smiled at her friend.

"Are you okay?" Addie asked. "Did you get hurt? Were you at your desk?"

"Addie, it's a really long story, the gist of which is I've spent the last three days in meetings trying to figure out how to rescue you! It's been a real experience. Once you're better and at home I'm coming over and giving you the details. I do have something to tell you, though."

"What's that?" Addie asked.

"The Speaker of the House is coming over to my place for dinner tonight. Can you believe it? I actually have a date!" Simone laughed.

"Girl, what are you doing here watching me sleep? You should be cookin.' What are you fixin' for the Speaker? He's a good man. I met him once when I served a luncheon for him. He made it a point to thank the wait staff, and honey that never happens.'"

"Addie, I was planning to cook. Then I realized about an hour ago I just can't do it; I'm too exhausted! So, I called this little Italian bistro around the corner from my house. I'm catering my first date with John McIntyre! That is absolutely pathetic!" Simone and Addie chuckled.

"I'm sure it will be fine. You better go home and fix up a bit. He's one handsome dude. 'Course, you're a mighty attractive girl. My, but this makes me happy. Are you excited?"

Simone blushed, and then said, "I am in between nervous, excited, and bushed! I just hope he's not upset that I didn't cook."

"Just tell the man the truth, that this is a down payment. You will cook just as soon as you can keep your eyes open long enough to read a cookbook! You better go, Simone. I'll expect an update tomorrow."

"May I tell you something?" Simone asked Addie. Addie nodded and Simone continued. "The thing is, I really like John. He is a solid, decent fellow. I just hope that . . . I'm good enough for him. I really want tonight to go well."

Addie looked Simone directly in the eye and said, "Simone Perez, listen to me. You are a wonderful, kind woman. He'll be darn lucky if you agree to a second date with him! The question is not whether you're good enough for him. No, baby, the question is if you'll agree to see him again. You're a classy lady. Your problem is you don't know you're classy! Go home and wear that hot pink sweater tonight. That'll wake the man up, for sure!"

They laughed together in the way exhausted people do. Simone leaned down, kissed her friend on the cheek, and went home to prepare for her evening.

On Thursday, Lillian arrived after ten o'clock, much later than usual. She had seen the good news earlier that morning and knew they had safely rescued everyone. Lillian briefly considered staying home and finishing up some loose ends next week. Yet, she knew the Speaker would need help with some of the details of firing Vaughn Hanesworth, and of course, she also needed to update him on her conversation with Congresswoman Albright. Lillian took a late train to work, telling herself she'd only work a half day.

When she arrived at her desk, Lillian noticed immediately that the Speaker's door stood firmly shut. Perhaps the Speaker's current conversation required absolute privacy. If not, he'd slept in. Either way, Lillian vowed not to disturb him. The Speaker would surface soon enough. Lillian opened her laptop and began sorting through her email and making notes for the upcoming week. She noted that John Sterling, with the House Office of General Counsel, had sent a detailed email explaining his citation of Vaughn Hanesworth. Moreover, the email explained that Mr. Sterling intended to seek compensation for damages done as a result of Vaughn's negligence. Everyone involved in this matter had signed off, and even Bob Harrington in the House Office of Government Ethics had found the time to sign off on the documents.

Lillian made a list of matters to discuss with the Speaker and was considering next week's calendar when John McIntyre opened his office door and asked with a yawn, "Lillian, when did you arrive? I must have fallen asleep. Let's get some coffee and go over a few things."

Lillian fixed a fresh pot of coffee and grabbed her notes. She brought two cups of coffee and sat down with her notes carefully arranged. "Mr. Speaker, the most important matter is a detailed email from John Sterling about Vaughn Hanesworth."

"I just read that. I know Simone Perez will be glad to see that email. Lillian, remind me to write him a personal note of thanks next week. He did an extraordinary job firing Mr. Hanesworth."

They discussed a few related matters, then Lillian filled John in on the phone conversation with Congresswoman Albright. John took off his reading glasses and twirled them absentmindedly, staring into space. He felt deeply sad she lost her baby. It would take her a long time to recover from this loss emotionally. Still, it pleased him that Janine might reconcile with her husband. He made some notes and then said, "Lillian, I'll call her and *The Post* over the weekend."

After they'd finished catching up on the week's loose ends Lillian asked, "Mr. Speaker, will the House take up the DOD Appropriations bill next Monday, and if so, will you be offering any amendments? I ask because if the bill will be on the floor Monday I'll work on amendments today, and take Friday off, if that's okay with you."

John looked at Lillian and chuckled. "Mrs. Hawkins, you don't miss a thing, do you? We'll take up the bill on Wednesday. The House Rules Committee has advised all members that they plan to hold an additional hearing on Tuesday morning. That means, Lillian, we have two whole days to take care of those pesky amendments."

Lillian gave an audible sigh of relief. She looked over her notes carefully, taking care not to miss anything. Finally, she said, "Sir, I see you're scheduled to address the Dundalk Chamber of Commerce awards dinner. Staff will finalize your remarks by Monday afternoon. Do you want me to do anything else to prepare for that? By the way, I spoke to the White House yesterday and rescheduled your call with the Chief of Staff for Friday morning at ten-thirty. Please let me know if that's acceptable, sir."

"Lillian, the speech next week will be easy. The White House call tomorrow at ten-thirty about the Civil Rights Commission is fine with me, although I'll probably take that call at home. I hope you're not planning to come in either, Lillian."

"No, Mr. Speaker. I think I'll take tomorrow off and come in bright and early Monday morning ready to tackle those amendments. Have a pleasant weekend, and please get some rest," Lillian said with a smile.

"I promise I will. Please give my best to Vern."

∼

John and Simone sat on the couch in her living room chatting. A bouquet of pale yellow roses interspersed with day lilies sat in a glass vase on the corner of her sideboard. John handed them to Simone when she opened her door, and simply said, "Here, I thought you might enjoy these."

Soon, they had devoured the manicotti, leaving only a small portion of sauce and a piece of garlic bread. John laughed at Simone's characterization that she had "catered" their first date. Their dinner conversation flowed freely as John told her about his children and grandchildren. They were obviously a huge part of his life. Simone regaled him with stories about her college years, trying to make ends meet.

Now they sat on her living room couch sipping decaf coffee. Simone explained she had played in a string ensemble in New Orleans. When John asked how she'd come to play in the group, Simone laughed and said, "When I moved to New Orleans, I didn't have time to look at homes, so I had a real estate agent rent me a small apartment in one of those beautiful southern homes. I'm moving in and carrying my cello up two flights of stairs when a tall woman of Creole descent opens the door and asks, 'You any good with that cello?' Not 'Hello.' Not 'I'm Reni Lescolette.' Just 'Are you any good on the cello?' I told her I gave it an honest try. Reni said, 'Great. Be at my apartment tomorrow at six. I'm in a string ensemble and we just lost our cellist. We get pizza; bring your own beer if you're into that.' Little did I know she'd become one of my dearest friends."

"Is she a professional musician?" John asked.

"No; actually, she's a phlebotomist," Simone replied. "I gather she's really good at what she does. Reni works for Tulane Medical Center and they've begged her to take a management position. However, she says that would interfere with her music. She's a superb violinist. Mr. Speaker—sorry, John—I promised I'd play for you. What would you like to hear? I'm fading fast and I fear if I don't play now, I'll fall asleep before I find the notes!"

"I have no idea," he said, shrugging his shoulders. "Just play whatever you like!"

Simone stood and walked over to her beloved cello. Dutifully, she rosined up her bow and then lifted the cello to her. "Under normal circumstances, I'd play Bach's 'Suite No. 1,' but that requires more energy than I have this evening. This is 'The Mission,' played by a popular group called the Piano Guys. I hope you like it." Simone said.

Then she closed her eyes and began to play the haunting tune with magnificent lilting notes. Her music filled the room, catching John off guard.

When she finished, Simone opened her eyes, yawned, and smiled warmly at John, hoping he didn't notice her mistakes.

"That sounded magnificent—wish it hadn't ended so soon." John said, stretching luxuriously.

"Well, I tell you what: I feel duty-bound to cook a real meal for you. Once I can keep my eyes open long enough. It's been such a long, tough week." Simone rejoined him on the couch and John put his arm around her. He kissed her gently, then said, "I have an idea. What are you doing Saturday?"

"Gosh, I'm not sure," she responded.

"My sister, Beverly, and her husband live on the Eastern Shore on a farm overlooking the Chesapeake Bay. Her husband is unable to help her much anymore so I go down there every few weeks and make sure they have what they need. In return, they let me keep my boat on their property. Anyway, I'm going down on Saturday. Why don't you come with me? It's a lovely drive." John said.

"Wait, you have a boat? Seriously?" Simone's eyes were wide.

"Play your cards right and I'll take you sailing in the spring. I've been sailing since I was a boy. There's nothing like a day on the Chesapeake! So, are you free on Saturday?" John asked, hoping he didn't seem too pushy.

"John, that sounds lovely. When shall I be ready to go? Will your sister mind me tagging along with you?" Simone asked.

"I'll pick you up at ten-thirty. That way we can both catch up on some sleep. Beverly won't mind you coming with me in the least, although I must remember to let her know. She's not one for surprises!" John explained as he stood to leave.

They walked to the door and John put his arms around her. He held her for a long time as she nestled against his shoulder. Then he kissed her and said, "I'll see you Saturday morning. Rest well, Simone. Thank you for dinner!"

Simone replied, "Thank you, John! See you Saturday." She closed the door and smiled to herself. Yawning, she picked up the empty coffee mugs and put them in the sink. Turning off the downstairs lights, she climbed the stairs to her bedroom, thinking what a lovely evening it had been.

Addie was absolutely right: John McIntyre was a good man.

Epilogue

BILLY DREXLER HAD NEARLY finished dressing. After much consideration, he opted for a striped business shirt, navy tie with matching sport coat, and freshly pressed khakis. He had begun working as the Special Assistant to the Architect of the Capitol six months ago. Today marked his first meeting with a new contractor, Turner Associates. This company was widely regarded and Billy vowed to look the part.

His life had turned upside down on the day of the explosion, nearly ten months ago to the day. Most of what had happened during those three horrible days remained a blur. His mind retained only snippets of events: a blinding flash of light, the searing pain as the pipe crushed his leg, the soothing voice of his beloved grandmother, long since dead. He awoke days later in Washington Hospital Center, his life forever altered.

Now, he sat on the bed and fastened his prosthesis to what remained of his left leg. In rehab, Billy had paid careful attention to everything they said, especially to how to get his prosthesis on and off, precautionary steps to take to avoid infection of the stump, and ways to manage the pain. He had learned his lessons well.

He finished attaching his prosthesis, which he had nicknamed Joe, and pulled up his slacks. He took a few tentative steps on Joe: step, clomp, step, clomp. He wondered if he'd ever get used to the sound of his own mismatched steps. He threw a quick glance down to make sure his shoes matched. A couple of weeks ago he had met a couple of buddies for drinks. Things were going well until Billy glanced down, only to realize he had a loafer on his right foot and a tennis shoe on Joe. He was mortified.

Billy grabbed his keys and headed for the door. He would not keep his new boss waiting.

∾

The first meeting with Turner Associates was endless. The staff of the new contractor sought to quibble with virtually every section of the new contract. Finally, Simone interrupted and said, "Ladies and gentlemen, perhaps we should reschedule this meeting to give you more time to rethink this contract."

Her comments had the desired effect. Within ten minutes, they signed the contract and the Turner staff left to hail cabs back to their posh offices somewhere on K Street. After the team had filed out of the room, Simone turned to Billy as she gathered up her papers.

"Let's go grab lunch and talk about the next steps for our new friends at Turner!"

Had it been anyone else, Billy would have begged off. Long walks were still painful. Still, Simone was his boss, so he just quipped, "Lead on!"

As they sat down at a cafeteria table Simone asked, "We were so busy preparing for this morning's meeting I forgot to ask you, how was your weekend?"

"Oh, it was really nice! Dom and his wife had me over for dinner Saturday night! His family gave him a telescope as a retirement gift. Man, he loves it. He often stays up late just watching the heavens."

"That makes me happy," said Simone. "I must call him. He's a good guy, for sure."

"Simone, I don't think I ever told you, but Dom blamed himself for the explosion. As I explained during our final interview—I'm the one who was responsible. Still, Dom felt like it came down to him for what happened. It's taken a while, but we've helped each other work through stuff. Now he's like a second father to me."

"So," Billy concluded, "that was my weekend—how was yours?"

Simone grinned from ear to ear and said, "Billy, how good are you at keeping secrets?"

"What you tell me stays between us—no matter what," he replied without hesitation.

"My weekend was fairly routine. Did laundry, cleaned my house, agreed to marry the Speaker of the House." She giggled like a schoolgirl.

Billy's eyes grew wide as saucers. "Wow! Congratulations! Man, that's really big news. I'll keep your confidence, but it's gonna be tough. When is this going to happen?"

"Well, that's just it. We want to be married right away—we even toyed with the idea of eloping. However, he's sixty-four and I'm forty-nine—that's a pointless exercise. I'm hoping we can set the date by Wednesday. I'll certainly let you know."

After they'd finished eating, Simone outlined specific tasks for Billy to complete on the Turner contract. Then she said, "Billy, you've worked for me four months now. I'm delighted with your work thus far. You learn fast, you ask thoughtful questions, and you're always eager to help your colleagues. Now that you've been on the job a while, I must ask—are there any accommodations you need that you may not have been aware of before you started? Before I give you a chance to answer, let me say that I don't have a problem with you teleworking one or more days per week. Just send me an email telling me what you'll be working on and giving a number where we can reach you. That's all that I require," Simone said. She sat back and looked at him inquiringly.

Billy thought for a moment, then said, "Gosh, I really appreciate that! Truth is, I did do too much walking this weekend. It'd be super if I could work on the Turner contract tomorrow from home. Is that fair to everyone else? I really don't want special treatment. Anyway, shouldn't I use sick leave or something?"

"First of all, this isn't special treatment. In fact, a good number of your colleagues work at home all the time. Second, I don't want you taking unnecessary risks. If you're home sick or have medical appointments, of course use your sick leave. On days like tomorrow—just take your laptop with you. Tell everyone what you're working on and how to reach you. Please see Stan the IT guy and he'll give you the software to log on to the office network. Then, voila! You just became a twenty-first century employee!"

Simone glanced at her watch and jumped to her feet, "Oops, I better get back to the office. I have another meeting in less than ten minutes." She slid her tray into the mobile racks and said, "Talk to you later, Billy!"

Simone's afternoon was a blur of meetings and phone calls. She didn't even have a minute to call John. To make matters worse, he had an important dinner meeting that evening with several Committee Chairs about several contentious matters. Simone had called Addie Hutchison over the weekend and planned to head to her house directly from work. Then her phone rang.

"Hello, Simone, honey. I'll be quick because you're at work. Listen, don't come over tonight. James and Jamal had a tummy bug over the weekend. Well, now I've got it too. Honey, it's nasty. I'll see you next week."

"Can I come over and take care of the boys? They'll need to eat." Simone said, worried about her friend.

"James still has a fever and Jamal is eating toast and ginger ale. Tyrone's been working hard on some project—he's been staying with Mr. Joel on the Hill. I'm hoping he can avoid this bug. Look, I'll call you in a couple days. Bye now."

For a few minutes, Simone sat at her desk feeling a bit sorry for herself. John was busy with work and Addie was certainly not in any shape for company. Simone had wanted to share her big news with Addie and enlist her help with the wedding plans. Now, that would have to wait. Given all Addie had been through, she was doing very well, Simone thought to herself. Senate Food Services had given Addie an early retirement. At first, she had balked. Then she realized: she finally had time for her grandsons and herself. Her health gradually improved and she'd begun to actually enjoy life. Simone chuckled, remembering when Addie took a cruise to the Bahamas with her church friends. "Hey, this is what we retirees do. We have a little fun! Plus, I am tired of these boys. Maybe they'll appreciate me more when I get back!"

Simone turned to her computer and dashed off an all-staff email explaining that she'd be working from home tomorrow and taking several conference calls throughout the day. Just as she turned off her computer, she received a text from John. "Honey—hectic day dealing with the lunatic fringe in House. All I know is this—I'll be home as quickly as I can. I love you!"

She turned off the lights and stepped out of the office, making only a quick stop on her way home to pick up a Philly steak with all the works from her favorite little hole-in-the-wall dive.

Then she headed home, donning her favorite sweats and devouring her dinner as she happily surfed the web looking for wedding ideas. Nothing quite suited her. Her busy day began to catch up to her so she closed her computer, yawning, and put her milk glass in the sink.

She walked into her living room and reached for her cello. She always took comfort in the feel of smooth wood beneath her fingertips, the scent of her rosined bow, the tentative sounds of strings in need of tuning. She took her cello and without even thinking, began to play "Jesu, Joy of Man's Desiring." She closed her eyes and felt the resonance of the music flowing through her. An overwhelming sense of gratitude welled up deep within her. She felt a sense of hope, a hope she had never felt so intensely.

For the first time in her life, her future—no matter what it held—gleamed bright before her. Bright indeed!